THE CHEF

MARTIN SUTER

THE CHEF

TRANSLATED FROM THE GERMAN BY
JAMIE BULLOCH

Atlantic Books
London

First published in Germany and Switzerland in 2010 by Diogenes Verlag AG Zurich.

First published in Great Britain in 2013 by Atlantic Books, an imprint of Atlantic Books Ltd.

swiss arts council

prohelvetia

Pro Helvetia supports and promotes Swiss culture in Switzerland and throughout the world.

10 9 8 7 6 5 4 3 2 1

A CIP catalogue record for this book is available from the British Library.

Trade paperback ISBN: 978 0 85789 291 1

OME paperback ISBN: 978 1 78239 061 9

EBook ISBN: 978 0 85789 292 8

Printed and bound by CPI Group (UK) Ltd
Croydon, CR0 4YY

Atlantic Books
An imprint of Atlantic Books Ltd
Ormond House
26–27 Boswell Street
London WC1N 3JZ

www.atlantic-books.co.uk

For Toni
20 July 2006 to 25 August 2009

THE CHEF

March 2008

1

'Maravan! Siphon!'

Maravan promptly set down the sharp knife next to the finely cut vegetable strips, went to the warming cabinet, grabbed the stainless-steel siphon and took it over to Anton Fink.

The siphon contained the paste for the wild garlic sabayon to go with the marinated mackerel fillets.

Maravan was convinced the sabayon would collapse before it got to the table as he had watched Fink, the molecular-cooking expert, use a mixture of *xanthan* gum and locust-bean gum – rather than *xanthan* gum and guar gum, as was advised for hot foams.

He placed the siphon on the work surface beside the chef, who was standing there impatiently.

'Maravan! Julienne!' This time it was Bertrand, the *entremetier*, for whom he was meant to be preparing the julienne vegetables. Maravan hurried back to his chopping board. A few seconds later he had finished slicing the rest of the vegetables – Maravan was a virtuoso with the knife – and brought Bertrand the vegetable matchsticks.

'Shit!' The scream behind him came from Anton Fink, the molecular maestro.

*

The Huwyler – nobody ever called it 'Chez Huwyler', the name written outside – was pretty full given the economic situation and the weather. Only a keen observer would have noticed that tables four and nine were empty, and that the reserved signs on two others were still waiting for their guests to arrive.

Like most of the top restaurants from the nouvelle cuisine era, this one was somewhat over-decorated. Patterned rugs, imitation brocade curtains, gold-framed oil prints of famous still lifes on the walls. The underplates were too large and too colourful, the cutlery too unwieldy and the glasses too original.

Fritz Huwyler was fully aware that the latest fashions had passed his restaurant by. He had detailed plans for 'repositioning' the place, as his interior design consultant called it. But this was no time for major investments; he had decided to ring the changes in small steps. One of these was the colour of the chefs' jackets, trousers and neckties: everything in fashionable black. The entire team was dressed like this, down to the commis chef, although the kitchen helps and office staff wore white as before.

He had also made a few tentative moves to push the food in a different direction: some of the classic and semi-classic dishes were accentuated with molecular highlights. So when the position of *chef garde manger* became vacant he had employed someone with molecular experience.

Huwyler himself had no more personal ambitions in this area. These days he helped out in the kitchen only rarely, concentrating instead on the administrative and front-of-house duties of his business. He was in his mid-fifties, a prizewinning chef many times over, and thirty years beforehand had even been one of the pioneers of nouvelle cuisine. He felt he had done his bit for his country's culinary development. He was too old to learn anything new now.

Since the messy separation from his wife – whom he had to thank for a large chunk of Chez Huwyler's success, as well the unfortunate interior decoration – he had performed all the meet-and-greet duties. Before they split up, he had found it a real burden to do the rounds of the tables, night after night; since then, however, he had warmed to the task. More and more often he would find himself chatting away at one table or another. This late discovery of a talent for communication had also led him to get involved with the Association of Restaurateurs, to which he devoted a lot of his time. Fritz Huwyler was a board member and the current President of *swisschefs*.

He was now standing beside table one, a table for six which had been set for only two that evening. Eric Dalmann was there with a business acquaintance from Holland. As an aperitif, Dalmann had ordered a 2005 Thomas Studach chardonnay from Malans at 120 francs, instead of his usual bottle of Krug Grande Cuvée at 420. But that was his only concession to the economic crisis. As always he had chosen the *Menu Surprise*.

'What about you? Are you feeling any effects of the crisis?' asked Dalmann.

'None at all,' Huwyler lied.

'Quality is crisis-proof,' Dalmann replied, lifting his hands to make room for the plate covered by the heavy cloche which the waitress brought to the table.

All this cloche business was something else he'd get rid of soon, Huwyler thought, before the young woman gripped a brass knob with each hand and raised the silver domes.

'Marinated mackerel fillet on a bed of fennel hearts with wild garlic sabayon,' she announced.

Neither of the two men looked at their plates; their eyes were fixed on her.

Only Huwyler stared at the wild garlic sabayon, a green sludge flooding the plates.

Andrea had become used to the effect she had on men. For the most part she found it tiresome; just occasionally it was quite useful and she would exploit it – especially when looking for work. This was a frequent occurrence in her life, because her appearance did not only make it easy for her to find a job; it made it hard to keep one.

She had not been at the Huwyler for ten days, but already she could see developing those familiar and tiresome petty rivalries in the kitchen and among the waiting staff. In the past she had tried to react in a friendly, jokey way. But on each occasion this had led to misunderstandings. These days she would keep her distance from everybody equally. It earned her the reputation of being stuck up, which was something she could live with.

'The food was better when his wife was still here,' Dalmann remarked when he and his guest were alone again.

'Did she take care of the kitchen too?'

'No, but he did.'

Van Genderen laughed and tried the fish. He was the Number Two at an international firm based in Holland, one of the largest suppliers in the solar industry. He was meeting Dalmann because the man could get him certain contacts. Putting people in touch with each other was one of Dalmann's specialities.

Dalmann had turned sixty-four a few weeks previously, and he bore the traces of a life in business where cuisine had always been a key instrument of persuasion: a little excess weight to which he tried to give some shape with a waistcoat, bags under his watery, pale-blue eyes, droopy, large-pored skin on his face, somewhat reddish over the cheekbones, narrow lips and a voice that had boomed ever louder as the years passed. All that remained of his yellowy blond hair was a semi-circular patch reaching below the collar at the back; to the sides it turned into two dense, medium-length cutlets, in the same greying-yellow tone as his eyebrows.

Dalmann had always been what today would be called a networker. He systematically cultivated contacts, brokered deals, gave and got tips, brought people together, gathered information and passed it on again selectively, knew when to keep quiet and when to talk. That is how he made a living, and a pretty good one at that.

At the moment Dalmann was keeping quiet. And while van Genderen talked at him in his gurgling Dutch accent, he discreetly looked around the restaurant to see who else was in the Huwyler that evening.

The media were represented by two board members (each with a female companion) of one of the big publishing houses that had recently been in the news on account of its drastic cost-cutting measures. Politics was represented by a party politician who had somewhat fallen into obscurity, with his wife and two younger couples, probably fellow party members whom the leadership had instructed to celebrate the older man's birthday. Medicine could boast the director of a clinic, who was in serious discussion with a senior doctor. At the neighbouring table a high-ranking official of a crisis-hit football club, currently without a sponsor, was dining with the finance director of an insurance firm, both men accompanied by their wives. In addition to these there were a car importer, the owner of an advertising agency and the former chairman of a bank whose resignation had not been wholly voluntary. All of these were sitting with their tall, thin, blonde second wives.

The room was filled with the comforting murmur of quiet voices, the delicate clinking and clanking of cutlery and the unobtrusive aromas of carefully composed dishes. The lighting was warm and flattering, and the torrents of rain which towards evening had started turning the fresh fall of late snow into grey slush could be heard only by diners with window seats. Even for them it was no more than a distant rustling through the curtains. It was as if that evening the Huwyler had cocooned itself against the world outside.

The world outside was looking pretty ugly. The day of reckoning had finally come for the financial markets, who had been dealing for years in fool's gold. Unsinkable banks were now sending out SOS calls as they listed heavily. Every day, more and more sectors of the economy were getting sucked into the vortex of the financial crisis. Car manufacturers were introducing short-time working, suppliers filing for insolvency and financiers committing suicide. Unemployment rates were on the rise everywhere, countries on the edge of bankruptcy, deregulators throwing themselves into the arms of the state, prophets of neo-liberalism went quiet and the globalized world experienced the beginnings of its first crisis.

And, as if it could survive this imminent hurricane by retreating under its diving bell, the small Alpine country started to shut itself off again. It had barely opened up.

Andrea had to wait until Bandini, the *announceur*, had scrutinized the dishes for table five and checked them against the order. She was watching Maravan, the nicest guy on her team.

By Tamil standards he was a tall man, certainly more than one metre eighty. Sharply defined nose, trimmed moustache and a bluish-black five o'clock shadow, even though he had arrived for the afternoon shift freshly shaven as ever. He wore a kitchen help's white overalls with a long apron like a traditional Hindu dress. The white crepe chef's hat looked like a Gandhi cap on his black hair, which was parted with precision.

Maravan was standing by the sink, rinsing plates with a hand spray to shift the remains of sauces, before stacking them in the dishwasher, moving with the grace of a temple dancer. As if he could sense she was watching him, he looked up briefly and revealed his snow-white teeth. Andrea smiled back.

During her short career in the catering industry she had come across a lot of Tamils. Many of them were asylum seekers with 'N-authorizations', which gave them the right to work in specific catering jobs for a low wage. Moreover, this was only permitted at the specific request of the employer, on whom they were more dependent than someone with a residence permit. She got on with most of them; they were friendly, unassuming, and they reminded her of the trip she had taken as a backpacker through southern India.

Since she had started at the Huwyler she had already seen Maravan working at every station. He was a virtuoso in his preparation of vegetables; when he shucked oysters it looked as if they were opening for him of their own accord; he could fillet a sole with a few practised movements of the hand, and was able to hollow out rabbit legs so carefully it looked as if the bone was still there.

Andrea had seen the love, precision and speed with which he composed artworks on the plate, or how skilfully he was able to alternate marinated wild berries with crunchy puff pastry arlettes to create three-layered millefeuilles.

The chefs at the Huwyler often used Maravan to carry out tasks that were their own responsibility. But Andrea had never seen one of them pay him a compliment for doing so. On the contrary, no sooner had he delivered one of his works of art than he would be redeployed as dishwasher and dogsbody.

Bandini approved the order; the two waiters placed cloches over the plates and brought them to the table. Andrea could now call up the next course for table one.

2

It was long past midnight, but the trams were still running. The passengers on the Number 12 were tired night workers on their way home and high-spirited revellers in a party mood. The area where Maravan lived was home not only to most of the asylum seekers, but also the hippest clubs, discos and lounge bars in the city.

Maravan was sitting on a single seat behind a man with a greasy neck whose head kept tipping to one side – a fellow restaurant worker, judging by the kitchen odours emanating from him. Maravan had a sensitive nose; it was very important to him that he did not smell of anything, even when he came home from work. His colleagues used eau de toilette or aftershave to cover up the kitchen smells. He kept his clothes in a zip-up, moth-proof carrier inside a locker, and whenever possible he would take a shower in the staff changing room.

Some kitchen odours he accepted, but these did not exist in the kitchens here. They could only be found in Nangay's kitchen.

Whenever Nangay dropped nine curry leaves – freshly picked by Maravan from the small tree outside – into hot coconut oil, the tiny kitchen would be filled with an aroma that he wanted to hold on to for as long as possible.

The same with the aroma of cinnamon. 'Always use more cinnamon than necessary,' Nangay would say. 'It has a lovely smell and taste, it's a disinfectant, helps the digestion, and you can buy it cheaply everywhere.'

Maravan had thought of Nangay as an ancient woman, but at the time she was only in her mid-fifties. She was his grandmother's sister. He and his siblings had fled with the two women to Jaffna after his parents had burned to death in their car near Colombo during the 1983 pogroms. Maravan, the youngest of the four children, would spend his days in Nangay's kitchen, helping her to prepare meals which his siblings sold at the market in Jaffna. Nangay gave him all the school education he needed in her kitchen.

She had worked as the head cook in a large house in Colombo. Now she ran a food stall at the market, whose excellent reputation spread quickly and gave her a modest but regular income.

Besides the simple dishes she made for the market, however, Nangay also secretly prepared special meals for a growing clientele for whom discretion was paramount. These were usually married couples where there was a large age gap.

Even today, whenever Maravan fried fresh curry leaves or simmered a curry on a low heat on his stove, he could picture a small, thin woman, whose hair and saris always gave off an aroma of curry leaves and cinnamon.

The tram stopped, a few passengers got on, nobody got off. When the doors closed again the man in front of him was jolted out of his sleep and rushed to the door. But they were already on the move. The fat man angrily pressed the button to open the door, cursed loudly and gave Maravan a reproachful stare.

Maravan looked away and gazed out of the window. It was still raining. The lights of the night-time city shone in the drops which traced slanting paths across the window. A man outside a nightclub was holding his head in the rain, his elbows jutting out. A few young people were sheltering under some overhanging masonry and laughing at his antics.

The party crowd got out at the next stop, followed by the fat man reeking of kitchen smells. Maravan watched him appear on the other side of the carriage and sullenly take a seat in the shelter for trams going in the opposite direction.

There were only a few passengers left in the tram, and it was obvious that most of them came from other countries. They were either dozing or lost in their thoughts, apart from one young Senegalese woman who was having a lively chat on her mobile, safe in the certainty that nobody could understand a word. Then she got off. Maravan watched her turn into a side street, still laughing and chatting.

It was silent on the tram now, save for the recording which announced the stops. Maravan got off at the penultimate one, put up his umbrella and continued walking along the same road. The Number 12 drove past him, the illuminated windows heading off into the distance, until they were no more than just another patch of light on the rain-drenched road.

It was cold. Maravan wrapped his scarf more tightly around him and turned into Theodorstrasse. Rows of grey houses on either side, parked cars, wet and glinting in the white light of the street lamps, the occasional shop – Asian specialities, travel agent, second-hand, cash transfer.

When he came to a brown 1950s block of flats Maravan fished his keys out of his pocket and went through a graffiti-filled passageway, past two overflowing dustbins, to an entry door.

He stopped in the hallway by the wall lined with pigeonholes and letterboxes. He opened the one marked *Maravan Vilasam*.

His post consisted of a letter from Sri Lanka addressed in his eldest sister's handwriting, a flyer from a firm hiring out cleaning ladies, election propaganda for a xenophobic party and a catalogue from a wholesaler dealing in specialist kitchen appliances. He opened the last of these while still beside the post box, and leafed through it as he climbed the stairs to his fourth-floor flat – two small rooms, a tiny bathroom and a surprisingly spacious kitchen with a balcony, all connected by a hallway covered with well-worn lino.

Maravan turned on the light. Before entering the sitting room he popped into the bathroom to wash his face and hands. Then he removed his shoes, put the post on the table, and struck a match to light the wick of the deepam, the clay lamp which stood on the domestic shrine. He went down on his knees, put his hands together in front of his face and bowed before Lakshmi, the goddess of prosperity and beauty.

It was chilly in the flat. Maravan squatted in front of the oil burner, pulled the ignition and let it spring back. The resonant sound of metallic hammering echoed through the flat five times before the burner ignited. Maravan took off his leather jacket, hung it on one of two coat hooks in the hallway, and went into his bedroom.

When he came out again he was wearing a batik shirt, a blue-and-red striped sarong and sandals. He sat beside the burner and read his sister's letter. The news was not good. Deliveries were being stopped at checkpoints on the border of Tamil-held areas. Very few of the food deliveries from February and March had reached Kilinochchi District. Prices of basic foodstuffs, medicines and fuel had risen exponentially.

He put the letter back on the table and tried to soothe his bad conscience. It had been almost three months since his last visit to the Batticaloa Bazaar, the nearby Tamil shop, to give money and his sister's ID number to the owner. It had been 400 francs, 37,800 rupees after commission.

Although he earned 3,000 francs per month, lived alone and paid a reasonable rent of 700, after the Huwyler deducted health insurance and tax at source, Maravan had just enough money left to eat. Or, more accurately, to cook.

Cooking was not just Maravan's profession, it was his great passion. Even when the family still lived in Colombo he had spent most of his time in the kitchen with Nangay. His parents had worked in one of the city's large hotels, his father at reception, his mother as a housekeeper. When not at school, the children were in their grandmother's care. But because Maravan did not yet go to school, his great aunt Nangay would often take him with her to work, so that her sister could do the housework and shopping. Nangay had six helpers in the large kitchen. One of them always had time to look after the little boy.

Thus he grew up among pots and pans, herbs and spices, fruit and vegetables. He helped to wash rice, pick over lentils, grate coconut, harvest coriander, and when he was as young as three he was allowed, under supervision, to chop tomatoes and slice onions with a sharp knife.

From an early age Maravan was fascinated by the process of transforming a few raw ingredients into something quite different. Something not merely edible, not merely filling and nourishing, but – something which could even make you happy.

Maravan would watch carefully, taking note of ingredients, quantities, preparation techniques and sequences. At the age of five he could already cook entire menus, and at six, before he was meant to start school, he learnt how to read and write because he could no longer keep all the recipes in his head.

For Maravan the first day at school was almost an even greater tragedy than the death of his parents shortly afterwards, the details of which he did not discover until he was almost an adult. As far as he was concerned, all that had happened was that they had not come to Jaffna with the rest of the family; most of the time they had not been around anyway. He found the journey to Jaffna chaotic and his relatives' house, where they stayed initially, small and cramped. But he did not have to go to school and could spend his days in the kitchen with Nangay.

*

The oil burner had brought some warmth into the small sitting room. Maravan got up and went into the kitchen.

Four fluorescent bulbs bathed the room in white light. It contained a large fridge and a freezer of the same size, a gas stove with four burners, a double sink, a work table and a wall unit covered with stainless steel, on top of which were various appliances and food processors. The room was spanking clean and resembled a laboratory more than a kitchen. Only by taking a closer look could you see that the various units were not all exactly the same height and that they had slightly different fronts. Maravan had bought each one individually, either second-hand from markets or from specialist exchanges, and installed them with the help of one of his compatriots, who had been a plumber back in Sri Lanka and who worked here as a warehouse assistant.

He put a small frying pan on the lowest flame, poured in some coconut oil and opened the door to the balcony. Almost all the windows opposite were dark; the back courtyard far below him lay silent and abandoned. It was still raining – heavy, cold drops. He left the balcony door slightly ajar.

Pots with mini curry trees were lined up in his bedroom, each with its bamboo cane and each a different age. The largest reached up to his armpits. He had got it as a sapling some years back from another Sri Lankan. Taking cuttings from this plant he had raised one tree after another, until he had so many that he could sell the odd one. He did not like doing this, but when winter came he did not have enough space. The mini trees were

He could smell the curry leaves, the cinnamon, the coconut oil. But he could not find what he was looking for: the essence of what these three things had combined to produce in Nangay's iron pan over the wood fire.

Maravan took a *tawa*, a heavy iron pan, from the wall and put it on the gas. He sprinkled some flour on to the work surface beside the stove and made a few chapattis out of the dough. When the pan was hot enough, he put the first one in, browning it on both sides. Another aroma rose up from the pan, which transported him back to his childhood.

When Maravan was fifteen, Nangay sent him to Kerala in southern India. An old friend of hers was working there as an Ayurvedic chef in a newly opened hotel complex, the first in the country offering a broad range of Ayurvedic treatments. Maravan would work in the hotel kitchen and be initiated into Ayurvedic cuisine.

He had already learnt a lot from Nangay and made little effort to hide this. Like a child starting school who can already read and write, he got on the nerves of his teachers and fellow students with all his knowledge. Although they lived on top of each other in the cramped staff quarters, he could find little in common with his colleagues and superiors. Even Nangay's friend distanced herself from him. She feared that he might have a more difficult time if he were seen as her protégé.

For the most part Maravan kept himself to himself, focusing on learning; this made him even more unpopular. In his spare time he would take long walks along the unending beach where not a soul could be seen. Or he would spend hours practising his elegant dives into the waves that rolled in unremittingly from the Indian Ocean.

In Kerala Maravan became a loner. And had remained one ever since.

The chapattis were ready. He took one, drizzled a little of the fresh concentrate on it, closed his eyes, and breathed in the aroma. He took a bite, chewed it carefully, then, instead of swallowing, pushed it to the roof of his mouth with his tongue and breathed slowly out through his nostrils – of all his failed attempts, he would give this one the second highest score: a nine. In a notebook labelled 'Extracts' he jotted down the date, time, ingredients, distillation time and temperature.

Afterwards he ate the product of his experiment as a seasoning on the chapattis, quickly and without much gusto, then washed the flasks and tubes in his kit, put them to dry on the draining board, turned off the light and went back into the sitting room.

On a small table by the wall was an obsolete, second-hand computer. Maravan switched it on and waited patiently for the machine to boot up. He connected to the internet and checked the auction for the rotary evaporator, which he had been following for some days. One thousand, four hundred and thirty, the same as yesterday. There were two hours and twelve minutes until the end of the auction.

A rotary evaporator would allow him to do precisely what he had unsuccessfully attempted again just now – in the correct time, at the right temperature, without any burning and no impairment of the taste. The only problem was that such a piece of kit cost over 5,000 francs, far more than Maravan could afford. Sometimes second-hand models were auctioned on the Internet, like the one on the screen in front of him.

Anything under 1,500 was a good price. Maravan had 1,200 put aside. And he could rustle up the rest somehow, so long as the price did not rise any further. He would sit tight for the next couple of hours and make a bid just before the auction closed. Maybe he would get lucky.

He took his sister's letter from the table and read it all the way through. She only came to the point on the last page: Nangay was ill – *Diabetes insipidus*. It was not real diabetes. She was thirsty all day long, drinking water by the litre, and had to go to the loo constantly. There was a medicine to treat the condition, but it was expensive and very hard to find in Jaffna. But if she did not take it, the doctor said she would dehydrate.

Maravan sighed. He returned to the screen. Still 1,430. He turned off the computer and went to bed. In the stairwell he could hear the footsteps of Gnanam on his way to the early shift.

3

A few days later there was a scene in the Huwyler kitchen which would have consequences for Maravan.

Anton Fink had created a starter which he called 'Glazed langoustines with rice croquant on a curried gelée', and which he wanted to put on the *Menu Surprise* for the following day. From the washing-up sink Maravan watched the chef preparing the curry sauce for the gelée: he sautéed some finely chopped onions, stirred in some curry powder and called out, 'Maravan! Coconut milk!'

Maravan fetched a tin of coconut milk from a cupboard, gave it a good shake, opened the tin and gave it to the *demi chef de partie*. As the latter was emptying half of the tin into the pan, Maravan said, 'If you like I'll make you a proper curry next time.'

Fink put the ladle beside the pan, turned to Maravan, looked him up and down and said, 'Oh right, a real curry. So some kitchen help is going to show me how to cook, are they? Did you hear that?'

His voice was raised and the chefs nearby looked up.

'Maravan here has offered to give me a cookery course. Maybe one of you would like to enrol too.' Fink had noticed that Andrea had come in holding her order pad. 'How to make a real curry. Introductory course for beginners.'

Maravan had just stood there silently. But now he noticed Andrea and said, 'I only wanted to help.'

'That's exactly what you should be doing, helping. That's why you're a kitchen help. You should be helping scrub pans, clean dishes, wash salads and wipe up spillages. But teach me how to cook? Thanks, but I think I'm all right, I can just about manage to put together a little curry on my own.'

If Andrea had not been there to witness the exchange, Maravan would have apologized at this point and gone back to his pans. But now he said bravely, 'I've been cooking curries all my life.'

'Oh really? Did you study curry? I'm terribly sorry, Doctor Curry. Or is it Professor?'

Maravan did not know how to respond. Breaking the silence that ensued, Andrea said, 'Well I'd like to try one of your curries sometime, Maravan. Will you cook one for me?'

Maravan was so astonished he could not answer. He nodded.

'Monday evening?' The Huwyler was closed on Mondays.

Maravan nodded.

'Deal?'

'Deal.'

Smoke was now rising from Fink's curry, and it smelt burnt.

Maravan suspected that Andrea's intervention would do him more harm than good. It had not only made Fink hostile towards him, but also stoked the envy of all the others. In spite of this, his heart was lighter than it had been in a long time. He blithely carried out the most mundane tasks and was not in the least bit bothered by the fact that nobody gave him anything more challenging to do that day.

Had she meant it seriously? Did she really want him to cook for her? And where? At his place? The idea of his receiving and entertaining a woman like Andrea in his small flat made him doubt whether he would really be happy if she had meant it seriously.

She left him stewing in this double uncertainty. When he was finally able to knock off from work she had already gone.

Hans Staffel had never been to the Huwyler with his wife. For business purposes he had been forced to eat in the restaurant two or three times before, and after each occasion Béatrice had made him promise that he would take her there, too. But Staffel was like all managers: the moment he had the chance of an evening off, he would rather spend it at home.

This time, however, there was no excuse. He had something to celebrate which, for now, he was able to share only with his wife. The chief editor of the most important business magazine in the country had told him in the strictest confidence that Hans Staffel was May's Manager of the Month. In ten days' time it would be official.

Béatrice did not know this yet. He wanted to tell her between the *amuse-bouche* and meat course, when the time was right and the sommelier had just refilled their glasses.

Staffel was the CEO of Kugag, an old family business that manufactured machinery. He had taken over twelve years previously and – in the words of the chief editor – regenerated the firm. He had convinced the owners to invest in a reorientation of the product range towards environmental technology, and to procure more capital by floating the company on the stock market. Kugag had bought a small firm with a number of patents for solar panel components and had rapidly become one of the biggest suppliers in the solar energy industry. Its market price had bucked the general trend by rising steadily, and Staffel himself had become a wealthy man. He had arranged for part of his salary to be paid in shares when the company floated, and these were still very valuable.

They had ordered two *Menus Surprises*, Béatrice's without any of the offal or frogs' legs that might appear in the various dishes. Out of consideration he had advised the kitchen of these requirements in advance.

The tall, pale waitress with the long, black hair all combed to the right had just brought the fish course: two giant glazed prawns on a rather nasty-tasting jelly. The sommelier poured out some champagne – they had decided to pass on the white wine and stay with champagne until they finished the fish course. It was as if this moment had been created for them specially.

Staffel raised his glass, smiled at his wife, and waited for her to lift her glass too. As she did it she knew she was about to discover what it was she had to thank this evening for.

At that moment somebody arrived at the table and said, 'I don't wish to disturb your celebrations, but I'd just like to offer my warm congratulations. Nobody deserves it more than you.'

He gave the startled Staffel, who had made to stand up, a friendly handshake and then introduced himself to his wife. 'Eric Dalmann. You can be rightly proud of your husband. If there were more like him we wouldn't have to worry about any crisis.'

'Who was that?' Béatrice wanted to know when they were by themselves again.

'I don't know. Dalmann, Dalmann? Some sort of consultant, I don't really know.'

'Why was he congratulating you?'

'I was just about to tell you: I'm Manager of the Month.'

'And of course I'm the last to know as usual.'

Maravan was busy putting away crockery when Andrea brought the plates back from table three. Fink rushed over to her, because he wanted to know what the customers had thought of his 'Glazed langoustines with rice croquant on curried gelée'. It was the first surprise of the evening.

The plates were empty apart from the heads of the langoustines and most of the curried gelée.

Maravan pretended he had not noticed. But Andrea looked at the plates with a disbelieving shake of her head, offered Fink a pitying smile, turned to Maravan and said, 'Is seven o'clock OK on Monday? Oh, and write your address down for me.'

The following morning Maravan was the first customer in the Batticaloa Bazaar. It was his second visit in a few days. The first time he had given the owner 800 francs for Nangay's medicine.

The shop was not well stocked, only tinned foods and rice, no fruit, hardly any vegetables. There were, however, posters and flyers for organizations and events in the Tamil community and a few LTTE stickers: the Liberation Tigers of Tamil Eelam. The Batticaloa Bazaar was less a grocer's than a liaison office and contact point for the Tamils in exile, and the first port of call for unofficial money transfers to the north of Sri Lanka.

Maravan went to work in a cheerful mood and kept up his good spirits in spite of all his team's efforts to ruin them. His rendezvous with Andrea had of course become common knowledge – Monday evening, seven o'clock, at his place! – and it was as if they had all sworn to make his life as difficult as possible before then: Maravan, fetch this. Maravan, fetch that. Maravan, do this. Maravan!

Kandan, the other Tamil kitchen help, was on duty. He was powerfully built, all brawn, slow on the uptake and without the slightest talent for cooking. And like many Tamil men in exile, he had an alcohol problem which he was able to disguise skilfully, although not from Maravan's sensitive nose. Today he was assigned all the more demanding tasks, while Maravan rinsed, scoured, cleaned, scrubbed and lugged stuff around.

An edgy atmosphere prevailed in the kitchen. There were few customers in the restaurant and a birthday party of twelve had cancelled their booking for the following evening. Huwyler was getting in the way, venting his bad mood on his chefs. And they passed it on to the *demis chefs*, who gave hell to the *commis*, who in turn laid into the kitchen helps.

But Maravan was on top form. The moment Andrea started her shift he had discreetly slipped her his address. She had smiled and said – loudly enough so that Bertrand, who happened to be standing nearby, could hear – 'I'm looking forward to it.'

Maravan knew what he was going to cook, apart from the odd detail which he would attend to the following day. And he also had a cunning plan for his technique of preparing the dinner.

Maravan was sitting in front of the computer with headphones on. Nangay's voice sounded weak, even though the connection was surprisingly good. He ought to have kept his money and let her die, she said reproachfully. She was tired.

Nangay was over eighty, and ever since Maravan could remember she had wanted to die in peace.

To begin with she was mistrustful and did not want to answer his questions. But when he said that it would allow him to earn more money, she listed ingredients and recipes, and freely explained everything to him in detail.

It was a long conversation. And by the time it had finished Maravan's notebook was almost full.

4

Happily, there had been a good number of covers at the Huwyler the following Sunday afternoon. The evening was quiet, the last diners left early, as ever on a Sunday.

Maravan was the last member of staff left in the kitchen. He was at the pan-cleaning sink, busy with the more intricate kitchen appliances: thermostats, jet smokers and rotary evaporators.

He waited until the cleaners had come into the kitchen, took the gadgets to the equipment store, then went into the changing room.

He deftly removed the glass elements of the rotary evaporator, rolled them up in two T-shirts, tucked them into a gym bag, making sure that they were well padded against the heavy main unit with its heat-bath holder and electronics.

Maravan undressed, wrapped a Turkish towel around his waist, shoved his underwear into the gym bag, took shampoo and soap out of the side pocket, and went into the shower. Five minutes later he came out again, took the clothes bag out of his locker, and got dressed.

On his way out he glanced again past the wine store. When he left the kitchen via the delivery entrance carrying a heavy gym bag, he was wearing black trousers, a dark-blue roll-neck sweater and his leather jacket. He did not smell of anything.

*

He got going that same evening. He broke up the panicles of long pepper into their tiny corns, deseeded some dried Kashmir chillies, measured out black peppercorns, cardamom, caraway, fennel, fenugreek, coriander and mustard seeds, peeled turmeric root, broke up cinnamon sticks and roasted all of these in the iron pan to the point at which the full aroma of the ingredients unfurled. He mixed the spices in various, carefully weighed combinations, and ground them into fine powders which he either used that night or kept for the following day, sealed in airtight and labelled containers.

The evaporator rotated well into the early hours with diverse ingredients: white curry paste, sali rice whisked with milk and chickpea flour, and – of course – the inimitable coconut oil with curry leaves and cinnamon.

Some fresh butter was clarifying in a pan to make ghee, while in clay plots warm water and grated coconut were being mixed into a milk.

Dawn was already breaking when Maravan lay down on his mattress on the bedroom floor for a short sleep full of strange erotic dreams. These were always interrupted when they got to the best bits.

Andrea had been on the verge of calling Maravan and finding an excuse to cancel. She cursed herself for her Good Samaritan syndrome. Maravan would have managed without her. Maybe even better. Perhaps her stupid intervention had only made things more difficult for him. No, not perhaps. Definitely.

Maravan was fortunate that these were the thoughts churning around Andrea's mind. Otherwise she would not now have been sitting on the tram, with her handbag and a plastic bag containing a bottle of wine on her lap.

She had decided to bring him a bottle of wine because she did not know whether Tamils drank. If they did not – and so did not offer any to their guests either – then she would be able to fall back on this bottle of Pinot Noir. Not a great wine, but decent enough. Probably better than anything a kitchen help could afford. If he had any wine in the house at all.

The reason why she had stood up for Maravan was because she could not bear those chefs, especially Fink. Not because she had the hots for Maravan. She would have to let him know this straight away, a diplomatic mission she was well practised in.

Her dislike of chefs grew with each change of job. Maybe it was because of the strict hierarchy that prevailed in kitchens. Because chefs behaved as if they had some sort of entitlement to the female waiting staff. That is how it seemed to her, anyway. In kitchens, even the humblest ones, a star cult prevailed which encouraged chefs to think they were irresistible.

Every day Andrea asked herself why she did not simply change profession. And every day the same answer came back: because she had not learnt how to do anything else. She was a waitress and that was that.

To begin with, she had wanted to manage a hotel or run a pub. She had started a course in hotel management, but got stuck in a traineeship as a waitress. She was soon fed up with college, and the possibility of working in a variety of hotels after a short apprenticeship – in summer by Lake Como or in Ischia, and in winter in the Engadin Valley or the Berner Oberland – seemed to suit her restless personality. If you looked as she did and knew how to get tips, the work was not badly paid. She had good references and experience, and had made it to the rank of *demi chef de rang*.

She had also tried out other jobs. One of these had been as a tour rep abroad. The job had mainly consisted of holding up a sign at Kos Airport bearing the name of her tour operator, allocating the arriving guests to the various hotel buses and receiving their complaints. Andrea soon found that she would rather deal with underdone or overdone steaks than missing luggage or rooms that had a view of the street instead of the sea.

Once she had even entered a beauty contest. She got past the first rounds and was thought to have a good chance of winning. Until she – the silly cow – had a moment of madness during a bathing costume photoshoot: when the photographer asked her whether she had ever modelled professionally before, she replied, 'Not with so many clothes on.'

Chez Huwyler was a well-respected establishment and would make a good impression on her CV. But only if she stuck it out longer than the usual few months. Half a year; a whole one would be even better.

On the other side of the tram, opposite her, sat a man between thirty and forty. She could see him staring at her in the reflection of the window. Each time she turned her head he smiled at her.

She took a well-thumbed free newspaper from the seat next to her and barricaded herself behind it.

Maybe she should try to start from scratch again. She was only twenty-eight; she could still start a course. She had her secondary school certificate, which meant she could go to art school. Or at least sit the entrance exam. Photography, or even better, film. With a bit of luck you could get a grant. Or some other government assistance.

Her stop was announced. Andrea stood up and went to the farther door to avoid having to pass the staring man.

Okra was cooking in a pan with green chillies, onions, fenugreek seeds, red chilli powder, salt and curry leaves. The thick coconut milk was still in a bowl by the stove. Maravan had decided on okra as a vegetable because of its English name: ladies' fingers.

The *pathiya kari* was a female dish, too: it was prepared specially for breastfeeding mothers. He had simmered some poussin meat in a little water with onions, fenugreek, turmeric, garlic and salt, added to this broth one of the spice mixes from the previous night – coriander, cumin, pepper, chilli, tamarind paste – brought the whole thing to the boil, then taken it off the heat, and covered it. He would heat it up again shortly before serving.

The male element of his menu was a dish of shark meat: *churaa varai*. He had mashed a cooked shark steak with grated coconut, turmeric, caraway and salt, and put this to one side. In an iron pan he had fried some onions in coconut oil until they were translucent, added dried chillies, onion seeds and curry leaves, stirring until the seeds started jumping, and taken the pan off the heat. Shortly before serving he would reheat it, add the shark-and-spice mixture, combining everything thoroughly.

These three traditional dishes were Maravan's proof that he knew how to cook curry, and an excuse for the other things he was creating on the side. He would make small, manageable portions and, as his one homage to experimental cooking, serve them with three different airs – coriander, mint and garlic foams – and curry leaf twigs glazed in nitrogen.

Maravan owned an isolation tank in which he could store liquid nitrogen for a short period. It had cost him a fifth of his monthly wage, but it was an indispensable aid for his culinary experiments and his efforts to outshine the chefs at the Huwyler.

What this dinner was really about, however, was the courses in between. Each one contained Ayurvedic aphrodisiacs, but in new, bold preparations. Instead of dividing all the purée of urad lentils marinated in sweetened milk into portions and drying these in the oven, he mixed half of it with agar. Both halves of the purée were spread on to silicon mats and cut into strips. The half without the agar was dried in the oven and twisted into spirals while still warm. He let the other half cool down and then wound the elastic ribbons around the spirals, which were now crunchy.

Rather than serve the traditional mixture of saffron, milk and almonds in its usual liquid form, he used cream instead of milk, whisking it into an airy mixture with saffron, palm sugar, almonds and a little sesame oil, and then put three heaped plastic spoons of the saffron and almond foam into liquid nitrogen, for just long enough to form spheres, which were frozen on the outside and soft inside.

He would serve them with sweet saffron ghee, which he spread on to strips of honey gel topped with threads of saffron, and then rolled them up. The saffron threads shone dark yellow through the opaque walls of these light yellow cylinders, which would be placed around the spheres.

He gave a new structure to the mixture of ghee, long pepper, cardamom, cinnamon and palm sugar. He mixed still water with the palm sugar, reduced this by half in the rotary evaporator with the spices, added alginate and *xanthan* gum, allowed the air to escape from the bubbles and made little balls with the portion spoon. He placed these in a mixture of water and calcium lactate. Within minutes the balls were smooth and shiny, and he injected a small amount of warmed ghee into each one. He quickly turned them to make the prick close up again. The balls were kept warm at sixty degrees. They were for dessert.

To go with the tea, he had prepared three varieties of sweetmeats, all made in the traditional way, of course, and all proven aphrodisiacs. He extracted the liquid from a pulp of sali rice and milk, and made a thick paste together with chickpea flour and sugar. He then added almonds, sultanas, dates, ground ginger and pepper, and worked it into a pastry, from which he cut little heart shapes. These were then baked and finally glazed with red fondant.

Maravan had steeped some dried asparagus in water, puréed it with the wand mixer and extracted the essence using the rotary evaporator. This essence was then combined with ghee and algin, and when the mixture had thickened he shaped it into little asparagus spears whose tips he coloured green with chlorophyll.

Taking the most popular Ayurvedic means of stimulating sexual arousal – a simple combination of ground liquorice, ghee and honey – he had created ice lollies by making patties, inserting wooden sticks, decorating them with chopped pistachios, then freezing them.

At twenty to seven he took a shower, changed and opened all the windows in his flat again. The only thing to smell of food should be the food itself.

5

On the short walk from the tram stop to Theodorstrasse 94 Andrea was approached by a junkie begging for money, accosted by a dealer and propositioned by a driver. She would book a taxi for the journey home, even if it was still early. And it would be early, she was absolutely determined about this. The moment she entered Maravan's flat she would tell him that she had almost not come because she was feeling so unwell.

In the stairwell it smelled as it always did in blocks of flats around this time of the evening. Here, however, the smell was not of meat loaf, but curry. On the first floor, two Tamil women were standing in the half-open doors to their flats, nattering away. On the third floor, a young boy was waiting on the landing; when he saw Andrea he disappeared into his flat, looking disappointed.

Maravan was waiting for her at his door. He was wearing a colourful shirt and dark trousers. He had just showered and was clean-shaven. He held out his long, slim hand and said, 'Welcome to Maravan's Curry Palace.'

He showed Andrea in, took the wine, and helped her out of her coat. Candles were burning everywhere; just a few spotlights here and there provided some more sober lighting.

'The flat's not nice if there's too much light,' he explained in his Swiss high German with a Tamil twang.

In the sitting room, a table no more than twenty centimetres high was set for two. The seating was provided by cushions and blankets. On the wall was a domestic shrine with a lit *deepam*. In the centre of the shrine a four-armed goddess was sitting on a lotus flower.

'Lakshmi,' Maravan said, making a gesture with his hand as if he were introducing another guest.

'Why has she got four arms?'

'Dharma, Kama, Artha and Moksha. Virtuousness, desire, prosperity and liberation.'

'Right, I see,' Andrea said, as if she now understood much better.

On a table by the wall an ice bucket stood next to a computer covered with a batik cloth. Maravan took a bottle of champagne from the ice bucket, wiped it with a white napkin, popped the cork and filled two glasses. She would have preferred the other scenario: no wine in the house; he would have had to open her gift, and she would have been able to talk about feeling groggy with a better conscience.

When they drank to each other's health she noticed that all he did was merely moisten his lips.

He pointed to the table. 'We eat special meals on the floor. Does it bother you?'

She briefly considered how he might take it if she said yes, then answered, 'But I am going to get a knife and fork, aren't I?'

It was meant as a joke, but Maravan asked in all seriousness, 'Do you need them?'

Did she need a knife and fork? Andrea thought about it for a moment. 'Where can I wash my hands?'

Maravan took her to his tiny bathroom. She washed her hands and did what she always did in other people's bathrooms. She opened the mirror cabinet and inspected the contents: toothpaste, toothbrush, dental floss, shaving soap, shaving brush, razor, nail scissors, two tins with Tamil writing on them, one yellow, the other red. All clean and tidy, like Maravan himself.

When she returned to the sitting room he had vanished. She opened the door to what she thought was the kitchen, but it was his bedroom. Also tidy, and with just a cupboard, a chair and a bed without a frame. On the wall was a poster of a white beach with a few coconut palms, their crowns almost touching the sand, and in the foreground a weathered catamaran. Along the opposite wall was a row of flowerpots with plants she did not recognize. On the wall behind the pillows a picture of the same Hindu goddess as in the sitting room, a few family photos, women of Maravan's age, children, teenagers, and Maravan with his arm around a small, white-haired woman. And an older, formal, retouched and coloured studio photograph of a serious-looking young couple, maybe his parents.

Andrea closed the door and opened another. She entered a room which looked like a miniature version of a professional kitchen. Lots of steel, lots of white, and pots, pans and dishes everywhere. It occurred to her now that this was the only room in the flat that had a smell, even though the balcony door was wide open.

Maravan came up to her with a tray. 'A greeting from the kitchen,' he said, realizing that this phrase sounded a little odd when uttered in a kitchen. They both laughed and Andrea went to sit down at her place.

The small plates contained five miniature chapattis and nothing more.

Andrea took one, smelt it, and was about to pop it in her mouth.

'Hold on.' Maravan took a pipette from a glass container on the tray and squeezed out three drops of liquid onto the chapatti. 'Now.'

Straight away an aroma rose from the tiny bread that was so mysterious and yet so familiar that she gave up her plan to make an early exit. 'What's that?'

'Curry leaves and cinnamon in coconut oil. The smell of my childhood.'

'And how did you capture it?'

'Chef's secret.' Maravan squeezed a few drops of the essence on all the chapattis. Then he sat opposite Andrea.

'You must have had a lovely childhood to remember its smell so fondly.'

Maravan took his time to answer, as if he had to make up his mind whether his childhood had been a lovely one. 'No,' he said finally. 'But the little of it that *was* lovely smelled like this.'

He told her of his time in Nangay's kitchens, the large posh one, and the small, crudely constructed one. Midway through a sentence he excused himself, sprang up from his cushions, nipped into the kitchen and came back with the first course.

It consisted of two intertwined brown ribbons, one hard and crunchy, the other firm but flexible. Both had been made from the same strangely sweet and earthy ingredients, but because of the fundamentally different methods used to prepare them, they tasted like day and night. Andrea could not recall ever having eaten anything so peculiar with such pleasure.

'What's this called?' she wanted to know.

'Man and woman,' Maravan answered.

'So which one's the woman?'

'They both are.' He poured her some more champagne – Bollinger Special Cuvée, on the Huwyler menu at 130 francs – cleared away the plates and went back into the kitchen. She took a sip and looked at his full glass in which only the odd bubble, filled with candlelight, rose from the bottom.

'And what's this called?' she asked when he placed the next dish in front of her.

'North-south.'

On the plate were three irregular pale yellow shapes, like sulphur stones. When she touched them they felt hard and cold, but when she copied Maravan and bit into them, the contents were lukewarm, light and airy, and the whole thing melted into something softer, more friendly, which had the sweet taste of exotic confectionery.

Surrounding these small ice spheres were gel cylinders in another shade of yellow, through which yellowy-orange threads of saffron shone in the candlelight. In the mouth they turned into another reward for having had the courage to bite into the lumps of sulphur.

'Did you make this up?'

'The ingredients are from an ancient recipe, it's only the preparation which is my work.'

'And the name too, I bet.'

'I could have called this one man and woman too.'

Was she just imagining it or was there a hint of suggestiveness in his voice? She did not care.

So far she had found it easy to eat with her hands, all the dishes had been as manageable as finger food. But now Maravan served the curries.

Three plates, three small portions of curry, each one presented on a platform of a different variety of rice, and decorated with an arc of foam and a glazed sprig.

'Ladies' fingers curry on sali rice with garlic foam. Poussin curry on sashtika rice with coriander foam. Churaa varai on nivara rice with mint foam,' announced Maravan.

'What's *churaa varai*?'

'Shark.'

'Oh.'

He waited for her to start eating.

'You first,' she urged him, and watched him use his thumb, index and middle fingers to form little balls from the rice and curry and put them in his mouth.

Andrea's first attempt was pretty clumsy, but as soon as she had taken her first mouthful she stopped focusing on the technique, just the taste. It was as if she could taste every spice. As if each one were exploding individually and the whole thing a continuously changing firework.

The level of heat was just right. It did not burn her tongue, was scarcely noticeable in fact, only revealing itself at the finish. It also acted as an additional spice, a final intensification of the taste experience, leaving behind a pleasant warmth which gently ebbed in the time it took for Andrea to prepare another mouthful.

'Are you homesick?' she asked.

'Yes, but not for the Sri Lanka I left behind. Only for the one I'd like to return to. A peaceful one. A just one.'

'And a united one?'

Maravan's right hand moved as if it had become disconnected from his brain and was now executing the task of feeding its owner independently. He had fixed his gaze on his guest and when the mouth spoke, the hand with its morsels waited respectfully and at a discreet distance.

'All three? Peaceful, just and united? That would be nice.'

'But you don't believe it's going to happen.'

Maravan shrugged. As if this were the sign it had been waiting for, the hand set itself in motion, placed a ball of rice in the mouth, and began to make another.

'For a long time I did believe in it. I even gave up my job as a chef in Kerala and went back to Sri Lanka.'

Maravan told her of his training in Kerala and his career in a number of Ayurvedic wellness resorts. 'One more year and I would have been the head chef,' he sighed.

'Why did you go back then?' Andrea was holding a morsel of

chapatti with coriander foam and could not wait to put it in her mouth. She had never realized how much more sensual it was to eat with your hands.

'In 2001 the United National Party won the elections. Everybody thought there would be peace, the LTTE called a ceasefire and peace negotiations began in Oslo. It looked as if finally we would see the Sri Lanka I wanted to return to. And I had to be there at the start of that.'

He dipped his finger into the finger bowl, dried it with the napkin, piled the plates, and stood up, all in a single flowing movement, or so it appeared to Andrea.

She watched him disappear into the kitchen. When he came out again a few moments later he was carefully carrying a long, very narrow platter, in the centre of which there was nothing apart from a row of precisely positioned, shiny balls. Looking like mini versions of old ivory billiard balls, they had the consistency of candied fruits, were warm, sweet and spicy, and tasted of butter, cardamom and cinnamon.

'And then?'

'I got a job as a *commis* in a hotel on the west coast.'

'As a *commis*?' she interrupted him. 'I thought you were almost a head chef.'

'But I was a Tamil, too. That wasn't a big deal in Kerala. But it was in the Singhalese part of Sri Lanka. I spent almost three years working as a *commis*.'

Andrea was already onto her second polished ball. 'You're an artist.'

'My chance came in 2004. The hotel chain I was with had turned a tea factory in the Highlands into a boutique hotel and they made me *chef de partie*.'

'So why didn't you stay?'

'Because of the tsunami.'

'In the Highlands?'

'It destroyed the hotel on the coast, and one of the Singhalese chefs who survived got my job. I had to go back to the north. And from there I watched how both the LTTE and government used all the world's relief supplies to advance their own political aims. It was then that I knew this wasn't the Sri Lanka I'd wanted to return to.' He was nibbling one of the balls now too, and put it back on his plate. 'And won't be for a long time.'

'But the tsunami was not that long ago.'

'A little more than three years.'

'So how come you speak such good German?'

Maravan shrugged. 'We've learnt to adapt. This includes learning languages.' After a brief pause he uttered the classic example of Swiss dialect: '*Chuchichäschtli*.'

Andrea laughed. 'So why Switzerland?'

'There were many Swiss people in the Ayurveda resorts in Kerala and in the hotels in Sri Lanka. I always found them friendly.'

'Here too?'

Maravan thought about it. 'Here Tamils are treated better than back home. There's almost 45,000 of us over here. Tea?'

'Why not?'

He removed the dirty crockery.

'Do you mind me just sitting here and being waited on?'

'It's your day off,' he replied, dashing into the kitchen.

A short while later he returned with a tray carrying a tea service. 'White tea. Made with the silver tips of tea leaves from the Highlands near Dimbula,' he explained, going back into the kitchen and bringing out a plate of sweetmeats for each of them. An ice lolly with sprinkles of green, surrounded by small asparagus with tips a toxic shade of green and dark-red, heart-shaped biscuits.

'I don't think I can eat any more.'

'You can always eat sweetmeats.'

He was right. The lolly tasted of liquorice, pistachios and honey, like something you might find at a funfair. The asparagus could be eaten like jelly babies and had an intense flavour of – asparagus. The hearts were sweet and spicy, with the aroma of an Indian market, and tasted – she could find no better word to describe it – frivolous.

All of a sudden she was aware of the silence that had descended on the room. The wind had also stopped blowing sheets of rain against the window. Something made her say, 'Would you show me some photos of your family?'

Without saying a word, Maravan stood up, helped her to her feet, and took her into his bedroom, to the wall with the photographs.

'My brothers and sisters and some of their children. My parents – they died in 1983, their car was set on fire.'

'Why?'

'Because they were Tamils.'

Andrea put her hand on his shoulder and said nothing.

'And the old lady is Na . . .'

'Nangay.'

'She looks like a wise woman.'

'She is.'

Another silence. Andrea's gaze wandered to the window. In the weak light that seeped out from the bedroom into the darkness, she could see snowflakes dancing. 'It's snowing.'

Maravan glanced at the window and then drew the curtains. He looked at her uncertainly as he stood there.

Andrea felt full and satisfied. And yet there was still a tiny hunger niggling away at her. Only now did she realize what it was she was after.

She went up to him, took his head between her hands and kissed him on the mouth.

April 2008

6

The following morning the news broke that the country's largest bank had to write off a further 19 billion francs, and borrow 15 billion more. It cost the bank's president his job. It was to be a bad day for Maravan too.

He had slipped out of the bedroom before six o'clock and made egg hoppers with *sothi* and coconut chutney. When he left the kitchen with the tray he almost crashed into Andrea. She was fully dressed.

He could think of nothing better to say than 'Hoppers?'

'Thanks, but I'm not really the breakfast type.'

'Oh,' was all he replied. The two of them looked at each other for a while without saying anything. It was Andrea who broke the silence.

'I've got to go now.'

'Yes.'

'Thanks for the fantastic dinner.'

'Thanks for coming. Are you on early today?'

'No, late.'

'See you this afternoon, then.'

Andrea hesitated, as if there was something else she wanted to get off her chest. 'Maravan . . .' she began. But she thought better of it, kissed him stiffly on both cheeks, and left.

From his window he watched her exit the building and trudge over to the tram stop, her hands buried deep in her coat pockets. A dismal day, but the street was dry.

Maravan went into the kitchen and did those same chores that were his responsibility at the Huwyler: scrubbing, washing and putting away the pots and pans.

It was the first time he had slept with a woman since fleeing Sri Lanka. And even the times before that he could count on one hand. Three times in southern India, twice in Sri Lanka; four of them were prostitutes, one a tourist. She was from England, around forty years old, and had told him her name was Caroline. But the tag on her suitcase had said Jennifer Hill.

This was also the first time he had felt good about it afterwards. No bad conscience. Without feeling the need to stand under the shower for hours. He was not surprised; it was the first time it had had anything to do with love.

Which is why Andrea's behaviour hit him particularly hard. Had he just experienced what other single Tamil men had told him about? Had he been exploited for a little bit of exotic amusement?

The morning was so gloomy he had to turn on the light to clean the rotary evaporator. He packed away the equipment, well padded in fresh clothes and the clean Turkish towel in his gym bag.

*

When he left the house it was raining again. It was still early and he wanted to be the first one there, straight after Frau Keller. She ran the administrative side of the Huwyler and worked normal office hours. She unlocked the delivery entrance at 8.15 on the dot. That would give Maravan enough time to put the rotary evaporator back in its place.

But then his bad luck started. He was standing at the back of the carriage, deep in thought about the night before and Andrea's strange behaviour, when suddenly the tram braked sharply, making a high-pitched screech, and came to an abrupt halt.

Maravan had not been holding on. He tried to stop himself from falling and in the process knocked into a young woman who had tried to steady herself by holding the back of a seat. Both of them tumbled over.

A few passengers screamed, then it went quiet. Ahead of them Maravan heard a car beeping its horn persistently.

He got to his feet and helped the woman up. An old man who was sitting down mumbled, 'Typical,' shaking his head.

The young woman had a *pottu* on her forehead. She was wearing a light-green Punjabi under a quilted windcheater.

'Are you all right?' Maravan asked in Tamil.

'I think so,' she replied, inspecting herself. From the right knee down her Punjabi had been dirtied by the muck left by passengers' wet shoes on the floor. The lightweight material of her gold-embroidered trousers was sticking to her lower leg and gave her modest appearance a touch of inappropriate vulgarity.

Maravan took a packet of tissues from his coat pocket and gave them to her.

While she was attempting to wipe at least some of the dirt from her soiled rayon dress, Maravan unzipped his gym bag and surreptitiously checked the glass flask rolled up in the Turkish towel. It was undamaged. He was so relieved he tore out a page of the notebook he used for recipe ideas and wrote down his address and telephone number for the young woman. In case she had to get the Punjabi dry-cleaned.

She read the note and put it in her bag. 'Sandana,' she said. 'I'm Sandana.'

They said no more after that. Sandana kept her head bowed, and Maravan could only see the beginnings of a centre parting under her hood. And the ends of her eyelashes.

The passengers were getting restless. One young man at the front of the carriage opened the ventilation pane above the window and shouted, 'Oi! There's people in here who've got to get to work!'

Shortly afterwards came an announcement from the control room: 'There's been a collision in Blechstrasse. Tramline twelve is suspended in both directions. The service will be replaced by buses, but passengers should expect delays.'

The doors of the tram carriage were still closed. Police and ambulance sirens got louder and louder, before stopping abruptly beside the tram.

Again it was the young man who had voiced his protest through the ventilation window. He took the matter in hand, opened the emergency exit and got off. The other passengers followed him, tentatively at first, but then ever more quickly. The carriage was empty within less than a minute.

Maravan and Sandana were the last to get out. At the doors Maravan said, 'I've got to hurry. I'm late already. Goodbye!'

'*Meendum Santhipom*,' she repeated. A delivery van had smashed into the front of the tram. One paramedic was bent over the open passenger window. Another was holding a drip bottle, from which a tube stretched through the window. Fire engine sirens were wailing in the distance. They were coming to free the driver from the wreck.

Maravan was the last to arrive at the Huwyler. He was almost late for his shift. Now there was no chance he could discreetly put the rotary evaporator back in its place. But he did have a plan B. When somebody needed it, they would shout, 'Maravan! Rotary evaporator!' because he was responsible for fetching delicate equipment. He would leave the door of his locker ajar, and on the way to the equipment store would pass by the changing room and fetch it.

The chefs greeted him with suggestive remarks. They all knew Andrea had been to his flat the previous evening. 'Hope you didn't make it too hot for her – the curry I mean,' one said with a smirk. Another: 'They say a real curry burns twice. Wouldn't hurt that ice-cold arse of hers.'

Maravan made an effort to smile and not answer back. But the atmosphere remained edgy. Even Huwyler made an unusually early appearance in the kitchen, getting in the way and referring to him as 'our spicy tiger'.

Maravan peeled potatoes, thinking, 'If only you knew, if only you knew,' when Fink suddenly yelled across the kitchen, 'Kandan! Rotary evaporator!'

Kandan had not even touched the rotary evaporator before. He froze, as did Maravan.

'Off you go. What's up?' Fink asked, casting a brief sideways glance at Maravan.

Kandan got moving.

Maravan's brain was turning over feverishly. Should he wait until Kandan came back empty-handed, and hope that Fink would send him instead? Or should he just go with him, fetch the thing, and hope that Kandan did not give the game away? Or should he say, quite calmly, 'The rotary evaporator's in my locker. I borrowed it'?

He continued peeling his potatoes and waited to see what would happen.

It was some time before Kandan came back. 'It's not there,' he stammered.

'Not where?'

'Not where it usually is.'

Maravan missed his cue. Fink hurried past him, past Kandan, and disappeared behind the door that led to the equipment store and staff changing rooms. Kandan followed him.

Maravan put the peeler and potatoes to one side and headed in the same direction, instinctively wiping his hands on his apron.

He could hear Fink cursing in the equipment store as he opened and closed cupboard doors and drawers. Maravan passed the store, went into the staff changing room, opened his locker and unpacked the rotary evaporator.

Behind him he heard Huwyler's voice: 'Today is the first of the month, so you've been paid. We're now going to see whether this machine's still in perfect working order. If so, Frau Keller will pay you the share of the extra month's salary you're due. If not, we'll repair it and take the cost out of what we owe you.'

The rotary evaporator *was* still in perfect working order, which meant that Maravan left the Huwyler with just over 600 francs in cash. While he was packing his belongings, the boss stood beside him to ensure he didn't try to steal anything.

As Maravan was about to leave, Huwyler said, 'You'll see. Summary dismissal from the Huwyler won't make it easy finding another kitchen job. You should count yourself lucky I'm not reporting you to the police. Otherwise it would be straight back to Sri Lanka.'

Andrea started her shift at four o'clock that afternoon. She did not know which she was dreading most: seeing Maravan or the rest of the team. But when she had changed and started setting the tables, nobody made any comments. Even during the briefing from the *chef de service* nobody mentioned her invitation to Maravan's flat the day before. And nobody said a word when she made her first appearance in the kitchen either.

It also looked as if she had been spared an encounter with Maravan. He must have been busy in the back of the kitchen, because she was never able to see him from where she was standing. He would be off-duty in an hour's time; she could easily keep out of his way until then.

The second time she went into the kitchen she noticed that Kandan was cleaning the pans, in the very spot where she had expected to find Maravan. That must mean he was prepping vegetables, as he did every evening.

But it was one of the *commis* who was cutting the juliennes for the *entremetier*. And doing it far less skilfully than Maravan.

It was still remarkably quiet in the kitchen, but now she noticed a few curious looks in her direction.

'Where's Maravan, by the way?' she asked Bandini, the *announceur*, who was standing next to her making notes on a menu sheet.

'Fired,' he muttered without looking up. 'On the spot.'

'Why?' Her question came out louder than she had intended.

'He borrowed the rotary evaporator. A thing like that costs over 5,000 francs.'

'Borrowed?'

'Without asking.'

Andrea let her gaze wander around the kitchen. Everybody hard at work, very deliberately. And in the middle of it all, blasé and autocratic, Huwyler in his silly black outfit.

Andrea tapped a knife against the side of a glass, as if she were about to propose a toast. 'I want to say something!' she shouted.

All heads turned in her direction.

'Maravan has more talent in his little finger than all of you in this kitchen put together!'

Then, seized by that impulse which had got her into trouble so often in the past, she added, 'That goes for the bedroom, too.'

7

A glorious April day. A procession of almost 2,000 children in colourful costumes and uniforms thronged through the city centre to the sound of marching music. Bringing up the rear of the parade was a horse and cart with a cotton-wool snowman, which was due to be burned ceremonially the following evening at six o'clock.

A little way outside the city a few hundred Tamils, also in colourful clothes, had assembled in their temple. They were here to celebrate the new year, which on this occasion coincided with the childrens' Sechseläuten procession.

They were sitting on the floor of the temple, chatting and listening to the predictions for the coming year, while the children played.

Maravan turned off the mixer, wiped his eyes with his sleeve and poured the contents of the glass container into the bowl with the paste of red onions, mustard seeds and curry leaves.

In an industrial-sized, stainless-steel bowl were some strips of green mango in their juice. Having combined them with grated coconut, yoghurt, green chillies and salt, Maravan now added the paste mixture, and poured over the ghee spiced with chillies and mustard seeds.

The neem blossom *pachadi* was ready. Using an old recipe, he had made it out of the bitter flowers of the neem tree, the sweet nectar of the male palmyra blossom, sour tamarind juice and spicy chilli flesh. A neem blossom *pachadi* should taste like life itself: bitter, sweet, sour and spicy.

After the ceremony the temple-goers would eat both *pachadis* on an empty stomach and then wish one another Puthaandu Vazhthugal: Happy New Year.

Huwyler had given Maravan the choice of a reference or a confirmation of employment. The former would mention Maravan's summary dismissal and give the reason for it (misappropriation of a valuable piece of kitchen equipment); the latter would note only the length of his employment and job description.

Maravan had opted for the confirmation of employment. But whenever he went for interviews they were always surprised that this was all he had to show for more than six months of working at the Huwyler. Afterwards he would either hear no more or get a rejection letter.

He went on the dole. At the end of the month he would get just over 2,000 francs. Plus whatever he earned unofficially.

This temple job was the first one of its kind, however. And it was badly paid, too. They had appealed to his community spirit and had expected him to do it for nothing, a sort of voluntary piece of community work. Finally they had agreed on the symbolic sum of fifty francs. The priest had promised to mention his name to the congregation. Maravan hoped that this publicity and the quality of the food would make him known as a chef.

The Sri Lankan diaspora was a closed society. Bent on preserving its culture and protecting it from the influences of the asylum country. Although the Tamils were very well integrated professionally, they shut themselves off socially. But Maravan was not a particularly active member of this community. He had not made any use of the services available to newcomers, except for the German course. He would go to the temple for the most important festivals, but otherwise he kept his distance. Now that he was trying to earn an income as a private chef, however, he lacked the necessary contacts within the diaspora.

The Tamil Hindus celebrated many religious and family festivals, plus ceremonies to mark the coming of age, marriage and pregnancy. They never scrimped on any of these occasions, and they all involved food.

Cooking for the New Year's celebration was a start at least. And – who could say? – word might get out in Swiss circles that there was someone who could deliver fine Indian, Sri Lankan and Ayurvedic food to your door. One day, maybe, in the posh part of town, you would find a delivery van – a turmeric-yellow Citroën Jumper, perhaps – emblazoned with the words 'Maravan Catering'.

And there was another dream he had: Maravan's. The only place to go for avant-garde subcontinental cuisine. Fifty covers maximum, a small culinary temple paying homage to the aromas, tastes and textures of southern India and Sri Lanka.

And when Maravan's had made him fairly well off, and peace reigned in Sri Lanka, he would go back and continue with the restaurant in Colombo.

There was always a woman in these dreams. But now she was no longer just a shadow, now she had taken shape and form: Andrea. She would supervise the service staff for the catering firm and work as maître d' at Maravan's. Later, in Colombo, she would just look after the house and family, like a proper Tamil wife.

But he had heard nothing from Andrea since that Tuesday morning. He had neither her address nor telephone number. After a week without any news he swallowed his pride and rang the Huwyler. She doesn't work here any more, Frau Keller told him.

'Could you give me her address or telephone number?' he asked.

'If she wanted you to call her, she'd have given you her number herself,' Frau Keller said, and hung up.

Maravan carried the bowls outside. By the entrance to the temple a large table had been set up under a colourful baldachin. Two women took the *pachadis* from him and started putting small portions on to plastic plates. Maravan helped them.

They were not even halfway finished when the temple door opened, the faithful streamed out, and each looked for their own pair of shoes among the mass by the temple entrance. '*Puthaandu Vazhthugal*,' they said to one another.

Maravan continued dividing up the *pachadis*, while the women arranged the plates. He focused on his work, but also listened with all the curiosity and anxiety of an artist to the comments at a private view. He did not hear anything negative, but very little praise, either. Cheerfully and without thinking, the congregation wolfed down all that he had prepared with such love.

He knew a few of the faces, but not many. Maravan's activities in the diaspora were limited to observing the most important festivals and contact with his fellow tenants in the block of flats, some of whom he would occasionally invite over as tasters. He would also pop into the Tamil shops and exchange a few words with the owners or customers. But otherwise he kept himself to himself. Not just because his work and lavish hobby scarcely left him any time. There was another reason: he wanted to keep his distance from the LTTE. They played an important role within the Tamil asylum population, from whom they obtained their funds for the fight for independence.

Maravan was not a militant. He did not believe in the independent state of Tamil Eelam. He would never say it aloud, but in his opinion the Liberation Tigers were making reconciliation more difficult and forestalling a return – maybe for generations – for all those who were freezing here and doing menial work. He didn't want to help finance that.

'*Puthaandu Vazhthugal*,' a voice said.

A young woman was standing in front of him. She wore a red sari with a broad golden braid and was as beautiful as only a young Tamil woman can be. Her shining, parted hair was set high on her forehead, her thick, barely arched eyebrows leaving exactly enough room for the red dot in the middle. The black of her pupils was only just distinguishable from the black of her irises, her nose was fine and straight, and below this a full mouth smiled a little shyly and a little expectantly.

'Did you get to work on time, then?' she asked.

Now he recognized her. The young woman on the tram. He had not noticed how beautiful she was when she was wearing the chunky quilted coat with the hood.

'How about you? Did the stains come out?'

'Thanks to my mother.' She pointed to a plump woman in a wine-red sari standing next to her. 'This is the man who knocked me over,' she said.

The mother simply nodded, looked from Maravan to her daughter and then back again. 'Let's go, your father's waiting.'

It was only now that Maravan noticed the daughter was carrying two plates and the mother just one.

'*Meendum Santhipom*,' she said.

'Goodbye,' Maravan replied. 'Sandana, isn't it?'

'Maravan, isn't it?'

May 2008

8

In May Maravan admitted to his family that he was out of work. He had no choice; his sister was begging him for far more money than he could spare. In Jaffna there were rice and sugar shortages. Even if Maravan had been working, what was available there on the black market would still have been beyond his means.

Nonetheless, he said he would rustle up some money somehow, and promised to call again the following day. But the next day he could not contact his sister. In the Batticaloa Bazaar he learned that Brigadier Balraj, the hero of the Elephant Pass Offensive, had died. Three days of national mourning had been declared, which many people in Jaffna were also observing.

He finally got through on the fourth day and had to tell his sister that he could not send more than 200 francs, scarcely 20,000 rupees. She was furious and reproachful – he had never known her to react like that before. It was only then that he came clean about his situation.

The month of Vaikasi was not exactly packed with festivals, and he had taken no bookings as a chef for family parties either. Job-hunting was a depressing process; not even hospital kitchens or factory canteens were interested in him.

If he had been in regular work, perhaps his romantic problems would not have bothered him so much. He would not have had to doze away his days in his flat, a lonely foreigner.

He was not merely lamenting a failed love affair. It had been the first time he had forged a personal relationship with anyone from this country. He had no friends, neither Swiss nor Tamil. He realized now that something was missing from his life.

Such was Maravan's mood as he drank tea on the cushions, in the same place where he had sat that evening with Andrea. The air was mild, the window open, the noises of summer resonated outside: music, the cries of children playing, teenagers laughing in doorways, dogs barking.

The doorbell rang. It was Andrea.

It had not been easy coming here. At first she was certain she never wanted to see him again. What occurred that night had profoundly shocked her. She had asked herself repeatedly how on earth it had happened.

The fact that Maravan had been fired the next morning made it easier for her to keep out of his way. She was, of course, sorry that she had been the real reason for his dismissal – she was sure this was the case. But she also felt that her act of solidarity had gone some way towards making amends. After all, her outburst had resulted in a summary dismissal too.

But she could not stop wondering how things had gone so far that night. The answer she found most palatable was that it must have been something to do with the food. Although this was pretty unlikely, it was an explanation that would not force her to rethink her whole life from scratch.

The more she allowed herself to recollect the atmosphere of that evening, the more detailed the reconstruction of her feelings and emotions, the surer she became that she must have been under the influence of something.

And yet . . . she had been perfectly conscious of everything. She had not been drugged or defenceless. On the contrary, she had taken the lead and he had followed. He had been willing, yes, but he had followed. It had been an evening and a night in which her senses had been arrested more intensely than ever before. She was loathe to admit it, but if events had been triggered by something beyond her control then it was all a little less complicated.

This was why, in the end, she had gone to see him on this unexpectedly beautiful May evening. She would turn up unannounced so he would not be able to make a fuss. She wanted to keep her visit as businesslike and as short as possible. In fact, she had given herself a small chance of avoiding the encounter altogether: if he was not home, then that was fate.

The newspaper she usually hid behind on tram journeys carried a report about the secret destruction of documents by the Government under pressure from the United States. They were plans for gas centrifuges which potentially could be used for the manufacture of nuclear bombs. The documents had been seized in a sensational case involving the smuggling of nuclear material.

Andrea read the story without much interest and peered out of the window, which was etched with amateurish graffiti, at the relatively empty street. Rush hour was over and the traffic of people on their way out for the evening had not yet begun. The tram was half empty, too. An overweight teenage girl had sat down opposite her and was patiently unravelling the earphones of her iPod.

A group of young, second-generation Tamil girls were standing outside Theodorstrasse 94, laughing and chatting in broad Swiss dialect. When they saw Andrea approach they lowered their voices and switched language. They made way for her and greeted her politely. As soon as she had disappeared into the stairwell, Andrea could hear them talking in Swiss German again.

The house smelled of stewed onions and spices. On the first-floor landing she paused, uncertain whether to go on or turn back. The door to one of the flats opened and a woman in a sari peeped out. She nodded to Andrea and Andrea nodded back. She had no choice but to continue. This was fate, too.

When she reached Maravan's door, she waited a moment before pressing the buzzer. She heard the bell ring inside the flat, but no footsteps. Maybe he's not here, she hoped. But then the key turned in the lock and he was standing in front of her.

He wore a white T-shirt with ironed creases on the sleeves, a simple blue-and-red striped sarong and sandals. Andrea had never seen him with such bags under his eyes, to match his bluish-black stubble.

He was smiling now. He seemed so happy that she regretted not having turned back on the landing. She could see that he was wondering whether or not to embrace her, so she made the decision for him by offering her hand.

'May I come in?'

He showed her into his flat. It was just as she had remembered it: tidy and well ventilated. In the sitting room the clay lamp was burning before the domestic shrine. As on the last occasion there was no music. Noises drifted through the window from the street.

A teapot and cup stood on the low table. She could see from the cushion at one end that Maravan had been sitting there. He invited her to sit opposite.

'Would you mind if I sat here instead?'

She pointed to the chair in front of his computer.

'Be my guest,' he said, shrugging his shoulders. 'Like some tea?'

'No, thank you. I'm not staying long. I just wanted to ask you something.'

She sat on the chair. Maravan stood in front of her. He looked nice. Neat, slim, well proportioned. But he elicited no feelings in her except sympathy and kindness. It was ludicrous that she had leapt into bed with him.

'Don't you have another chair?'

'In the kitchen.'

'Aren't you going to fetch it?'

'In my culture it is impolite to sit at the same height as one's superiors.'

'I'm not your superior.'

'As far as I'm concerned, you are.'

'Nonsense. Get a chair and sit down.'

Maravan sat on the floor.

Andrea shook her head and asked her question: 'What was in the food?'

'You mean the ingredients?'

'Only the ones that produced that effect.'

'I don't understand.'

He was a bad liar. Until then Andrea had harboured doubts about her theory. But now he was acting as if he had been caught red-handed, so she was quite sure. 'You understand perfectly well.'

'I made the meal with traditional ingredients. There was nothing in there that didn't belong.'

'Maravan, I know that's not true. I'm absolutely certain. I know myself and my body. Something about that meal wasn't right.'

He was silent for a moment. Then he shook his head stubbornly.

'These are ancient recipes. All I did was to modernize the preparation a little. I swear to you there was nothing in there.'

Andrea got up and paced back and forth between the shrine and the window. It was getting dark, the sky above the tiled roofs had turned orange; there were no voices to be heard from the street any more.

She turned from the window and thrust herself in front of him. 'Get up, Maravan.'

He stood and lowered his eyes.

'Look at me.'

'In my culture it is impolite to look someone in the eyes.'

'In my culture it is impolite to put something in a woman's food to make her sleep with you.'

He looked at her. 'I didn't put anything in your food.'

'Let me tell you a secret, Maravan: I don't sleep with men. They don't turn me on. They've never turned me on. When I was a teenager I slept with a boy twice because I thought that was what you did. But after that second time I already knew I'd never do it again.'

She paused for a moment. 'I don't sleep with men, Maravan. I sleep with women.'

He cast her a horrified look.

'Do you understand now?'

He nodded.

'So, what was in the food?'

Maravan took his time. Then he said, 'Ayurveda is a type of medicine which is many thousands of years old. It has eight disciplines. The eighth is called Vajikarana. It's all about aphrodisiacs. This includes certain food dishes. My great-aunt Nangay is a wise woman; she knows how to prepare such dishes. I got my recipes from her. But the way in which they were prepared was all my own invention.'

By the time Andrea left that evening, she had been initiated into the aphrodisiac secrets of milk and urad lentils, saffron and palm sugar, almonds and sesame oil, saffron ghee and long pepper, cardamom and cinnamon, asparagus and liquorice ghee.

She had given him a moderate ticking-off, even going so far as to describe his behaviour as 'Ayurvedic date rape', and she left his flat without saying goodbye. But now she felt more relieved than troubled. A couple of tram stops before she got off, when Andrea was able to look back at the whole affair with a little distance, she could not help laughing out loud.

A young man opposite her smiled back.

Their meeting had also brought Maravan some consolation. Now he could deal with the reasons for her rejection. He even felt a little pride at having been the only man for whom, for a night, she had betrayed her natural inclinations. And – if he were being honest – a little hope, too.

The following day he sent his sister 10,000 rupees to give him an excuse for calling her, and then he asked her to arrange a time for him to speak with Nangay. He would have to wait two more days.

When he finally got through to Nangay, she sounded weak and exhausted.

'Are you taking your medicine, *mami*?' he asked. He used the traditional polite form of the second person and called her *mami*: aunt.

'Yes, yes. Is that why you're calling?'

'Partly.'

'Why else?'

Maravan did not really know where to begin. She pre-empted him.

'If it doesn't work the first time, that's perfectly normal. Sometimes it takes weeks, months. Tell them they have to be patient.'

'It did work the first time.'

For a while she said nothing. Then, 'That happens if both people believe strongly enough.'

'But the woman didn't believe. She didn't even know.'

'Then she loves the man.'

Maravan did not answer.

'Are you still there, Maravan?'

'Yes.'

Nangay asked quietly, 'Is she a Shudra, at least?'

'Yes, *mami*.' The lie was excusable, he thought. Shudra was the servant caste. And Andrea was an employee in the service industry, after all.

When his sister came on again, he asked, 'Is she really taking her medicine?'

'How can she?' She sounded annoyed. 'We haven't even got enough money for rice and sugar.'

After the conversation Maravan sat in front of the screen for a good while. He was now convinced that the rapid effect of the food must be down to his molecular cooking.

June 2008

9

It had been so sunny on Sunday morning that Dalmann had taken breakfast on the terrace. But no sooner had Lourdes brought out the scrambled eggs and bacon than the wind blew a large cloud across the sun.

Dalmann got stuck into his breakfast nonetheless, and reached for the top newspaper on the pile of four laid out by the housekeeper. Now he began to feel gloomier. The hysteria surrounding the destruction of the documents by the Bundesrat had thrown up a lot of dirt, unnecessarily. A section of the Federal News Service's report about the nuclear smuggling affair had fallen into the hands of a journalist, and now they were talking about the Iranian connection as well as the Pakistani one. It would not be long before the name Palucron appeared in the newspaper.

Palucron was a company – now no longer trading – with its headquarters in a lawyer's office in the city centre. At the time it had channelled payments from Iran to various firms, all of them rock-solid enterprises with impeccable reputations, who certainly had no idea that they were implicated in the development of a nuclear programme.

Of course this was also true of Palucron, officially. At least it was for its director, Eric Dalmann, who had only taken up the position at the request of a business acquaintance to whom he owed a favour.

At all events, it would be extremely inconvenient for him to be mentioned in the same breath as this story, especially at a time when business was taking a knock due to the financial crisis.

Dalmann looked up at the sky. A whole bank of cloud was obscuring the sun. He was wearing casual summer clothes – a green polo shirt and light, tartan golf slacks – and an unpleasantly cold wind chilled him to the bone.

'Lourdes!' he called. 'We're going inside.' He stood, picked up his coffee cup, and went through the veranda door into the living room. He sat in an armchair, staring morosely, until the housekeeper had cleared the breakfast from the terrace and laid the table in the dining room.

He had scarcely sat down and started on a new plate of scrambled eggs and bacon – the first, only half eaten, had gone cold during the change of tables – before the doorbell rang. Schaeffer, as ever, was a little too punctual.

Schaeffer was Dalmann's colleague. Dalmann could not think of another word for him. He was not exactly a secretary or an assistant, and right-hand man did not describe him accurately either. So Dalmann had stuck with 'colleague'. They had been colleagues for nearly ten years now and had dispensed with formalities early on. Schaeffer called Dalmann Eric, Dalmann called Schaeffer Schaeffer.

Lourdes showed him in. He was a tall, gangly man in his early forties, with a narrow head, thinning blond hair and bright blue eyes. A few years back he had swapped his rimless glasses for contact lenses, which did nothing for his sensitive eyes; he was forever throwing his head back and squeezing drops under his eyelids.

Like Dalmann, Schaeffer was in casual clothes. A light-blue shirt with a button-down collar, dark-blue linen trousers and a red cashmere pullover slung carefully over his shoulders. In one hand he carried a heavy briefcase.

'I wanted to eat outside, but . . .' Dalmann pointed vaguely upwards.

'The outlook for the weather is not promising,' Schaeffer answered.

Dalmann took a mouthful and pointed to a chair where a second place had been set. Schaeffer sat and put the briefcase on the floor beside him. 'I hope it's not going to piss it down for the opening game.'

Euro 2008 was scheduled to start in a week's time. The ideal PR opportunity for Dalmann. Thanks to his UEFA contacts he had stockpiled tickets for the most important games and had organized events, either himself or through others – dinners in exclusive restaurants, visits to nightclubs, etc. – around the tournament. This was one of Schaeffer's most important jobs at present, and also the real reason for his Sunday visit.

But for the moment Palucron was top priority.

Schaeffer had already had breakfast. He drank a cup of tea and peeled an apple so carefully that it got on Dalmann's nerves. He pushed one of the Sunday newspapers across the table. 'Have you seen this?'

Schaeffer nodded and bit into a slice of apple. The care he took in chewing it got on Dalmann's nerves, too. Everything about

Schaeffer got on his nerves. But he was good, he had to give him that – which is why Dalmann had put up with him for so long. 'Do you know this Huber fellow?' Huber was the journalist who had written the article.

Schaeffer shook his head until he had swallowed his mouthful. 'But I do know his boss.'

'I know him too. We can always use our clout with him later. All we need to know right now is whether Palucron is mentioned in this report.'

'We have to make that assumption.'

I wish he wouldn't talk so pompously all the time, Dalmann thought. 'The paper's got an "extract" from the report. If Palucron were mentioned in this extract then surely it would be in the newspaper.'

In his hand Schaeffer held the slice of apple that was destined for his mouth. 'Or they're saving this detail for next Sunday.'

'Look, Schaeffer, that's why I want you to find out how much they've got.'

Schaeffer placed the slice of apple in his mouth and chewed thoughtfully. Finally he swallowed, nodded and said, 'I think that's within the realm of the doable.'

'Good,' Dalmann muttered. 'Then do it.'

They started talking about Euro 2008.

The following Sunday the same newspaper revealed further details about the nuclear affair. There was no mention of Palucron.

10

The European Championships had given Maravan a breathing space. The catering industry needed so many staff that even Huwyler's excommunication was no obstacle to finding a job. At least not for the owner of a food stall along the tourist strip.

Maravan was hired to do the washing up. He worked in the stiflingly hot corner of a tent, separated from the kitchen and serving counter. He had to scrub the pans and chafing dishes by hand; a dishwasher was at his disposal for cutlery and crockery. But it was so defective it kept on breaking down, and meant that Maravan was forced to clean these by hand as well.

It was monotonous work. Sometimes he had nothing to do for hours, and then, when an onslaught of hungry fans arrived, he could not keep up with the work. The boss held both of these things – doing nothing and not keeping up – against him. But only in the way that he held everything against everybody. He ensured that the work atmosphere was lousy; he had paid good money for a licence, expected to do fantastic business and now he had to sit through long slack periods in the tourist strip. Switzerland had been knocked out, and the weather was cold and rainy. Maravan was counting down the days till the end of the European Championships.

Not just because of the job. The hype was getting on his nerves. He was not interested in football. Swimming had been his sport. And when he was much younger he had also liked cricket – before he had devoted himself entirely to cooking.

The one good thing about this job was that the social security office knew nothing about it. A slightly dodgy temp firm, who worked mainly with people in his situation, had organized the job for Maravan. Although he was poorly paid, twenty francs per hour, this was in addition to his dole money.

He had taken out a loan – 3,000 francs – to send his sister money for Nangay's treatment. Not from a bank, of course – what bank in the world would have given credit to an unemployed asylum seeker? – but from Ori, a Tamil businessman who lent money privately. Fifteen per cent interest. On the whole sum until the loan was paid back.

To begin with he had tried to do it without a loan. As soon as he had heard that Nangay could not continue with her treatment, he had worked illegally at a used tyre warehouse. He had to spend the whole day sorting through heavy tyres.

But he did not last. Not because he found the work too strenuous, but because it was too dirty. There was no shower there and he could not get rid of the stink of rubber and the black filth at the wash basin. He could just about put up with the fact that he was slaving away at the very bottom of the social ladder. But his pride did not allow him to look or smell like it.

He had also tried his hand in the construction industry. He was working for a subcontractor of a subcontractor at a large building site. But on the second day an official turned up from the city authorities checking for black market workers. Maravan and two of his colleagues managed to disappear just in time. The subcontractor still owed him money.

In the washing-up tent he had no idea how chilly it was outside. Maravan was scrubbing the stubborn remains of goulash from a food container. Apart from that he had nothing to do. Through the side of the tent he could hear the voice of a football commentator. The Italy–Romania game was playing on the small television set. All the food stalls along the tourist strip were hoping for an Italian victory. There were far more Italians than Romanians in town and they spent more money too.

Finally, in the fifty-fifth minute, salvation arrived in the form of a goal: 1–0. The triumphant screams startled Maravan; he peeped through the curtain which covered the entrance to the stall. His boss was whooping loudest of all. He was skipping up and down with his arms thrust into the air, shouting 'Italia! Italia!'

Maravan pretended he was delighted as well, and this was his downfall. At the very moment he beamed through the curtain, Romania equalized. His boss turned away from the television in disgust and caught sight of Maravan's grinning face. He said nothing, but as soon as the game was over and the flood of euphoric Italian fans they had been hoping for failed to materialize at any point that evening, he paid Maravan and told him not to come back tomorrow.

Contrary to his usual habit Maravan travelled home in the front carriage of the Number 12 tram. A fan had thrown up in the rear carriage, and Maravan could not stomach the stench.

A few lone fans were still on the streets, making their way back to the city centre. The scarves in their teams' colours were now acting as protection against the cold wind, and only the occasional snippet of an anthem or chant could be heard from inside the tram.

Maravan had never felt such despair. Not even on the day when he gave his entire savings to a people smuggler. At least that had been a way out.

This time he could not see one. Or only a very humiliating one. If he had committed himself to the Liberation Tigers he would have got that job in the Ceylonese restaurant. The owner did not care that he had been booted out of the Huwyler. He would have taken Maravan on as a kitchen help, with the prospect of promotion to chef. But when he reacted to the crunch question of where he stood on the Liberation Tigers with a shrug of his shoulders, he knew in an instant he would not get the job. The LTTE was ubiquitous within the diaspora. Nobody who was reliant on the help of their compatriots here could afford to distance themselves from the Tigers.

Maybe he should go back. He could not have less of a future than he did here.

July 2008

11

A summer's day at the end of July; the temperature had risen above twenty-five degrees, although there was still a light northerly wind.

Barack Obama, the Democratic presidential candidate, spoke to 200,000 people in Berlin and promised them a change for the whole world. It needed a change: two days previously the second largest mortgage bank in the United States had collapsed, and several others were getting into ever greater difficulties.

The Sri Lankan army reported that the LTTE had suffered a heavy defeat in Mullaitivu District. And the LTTE reported on the third offer of an amnesty to deserters from the Sri Lankan army that year.

With a teaspoon, Maravan scooped one of the green split roasted mung beans out of the boiling water and tested it. It was done, but still firm. He poured away the water, spread the beans out on a silicon mat and left them to cool.

He added shredded coconut, jiggery and finely ground cardamom seeds, mixing everything thoroughly in a bowl. Then he worked roasted rice flour and boiling water into a stiff dough. The amount of water had to be just right: too much water and the dough would come together badly; too little and it would go hard after steaming.

Maravan washed his hands and rubbed them with some coconut oil. He rolled out little balls from the rice flour dough and made them into small vessels, which he filled with the spicy gram mixture, and then sealed them, making pointy balls. He steamed these, placed them in the thermobox, then set about making the next thirty.

Maravan had become the supplier of *modhakam*, the favourite sweet of Ganesh, the elephant-headed Lord of Hosts.

Every morning and evening he produced around a hundred *modhakam*, which the faithful could buy outside the temple and offer up to Ganesh. Temple-goers who had cars would take turns to pick up the full thermobox shortly before eight in the morning and just before six in the evening, and return the empty one.

The idea had been his own. To put it into practice he needed to increase his loan with Ori. He had to buy the boxes and make a donation of 1,000 francs to the LTTE. But now this also allowed him to supply Tamil food shops and two Ceylonese restaurants with biscuits and other sweet things. Business was not exactly thriving, but it was starting to trickle in. Maybe this was the first step towards Maravan Catering.

The doorbell rang. Maravan looked at his watch. It was only just past five o'clock; the temple courier was early today.

'Hold on!' he called out in Tamil. He washed his hands and opened the door.

Andrea.

She was carrying a bunch of flowers and a bottle of wine. She presented him with both of these. 'I know you don't drink. But I do.'

As with her previous unannounced visit, she had to ask, 'May I come in?' before Maravan snapped out of his shock.

He invited her into the flat. She saw the open kitchen door and his apron and asked, 'Are you expecting guests?'

'No, I'm making *modhakam.*' He went into the kitchen, took two from the thermobox, put them on a plate and offered it to her. 'Here you go. You can eat it or give it as an offering.'

'I'd rather give it as an offering,' she decided with a smile.

'I see. No, no, don't worry, it's harmless.'

Andrea did not take one all the same. 'Have you got any time at the moment?'

'Twenty more, then I'll have time. Do you want to wait in the sitting room?'

'I'll watch.'

When the doorbell rang Maravan was ready. This time the person taking the sweets to the temple was a plump, middle-aged woman he recognized. But he could not recall where he had seen her before. Maybe she would have told him, but the moment she saw Andrea in the kitchen her smile dissolved. She took the thermobox and left almost without saying goodbye.

'Can people order meals from you?'

They were sitting on the cushions at the low table. Andrea had a glass of wine in front of her, Maravan a cup of tea. Before he sat down he had ceremoniously lit the *deepam* by his domestic shrine, murmuring something while doing so.

'They can. One day I'd even like to make a living from it.'

'I mean a special meal.'

'I try to make each one special.'

She took a sip of wine and put the glass down slowly. 'I mean special in the same way that you made that dinner for me. Can people order that from you?'

Maravan thought for a moment. 'Something similar, yes.'

'It would have to be exactly the same.'

'But I'd need a rotary evaporator.'

'What would that cost?'

'Around six thousand.'

'Ouch!'

Andrea swirled around the red wine in her glass and pondered. She had a lot of connections in the catering industry. Surely it would be possible to get hold of one of those things.

'What if I were to hire one?'

'Then it would be exactly the same.' Maravan poured her some more wine.

'Exactly the same effect, too?'

He raised his shoulders and smiled. 'We could try it out.'

'Not "we", Maravan,' she said circumspectly.

12

Andrea lived in roughly the area where, in his dreams, Maravan had pictured the turmeric-coloured delivery van splashed with the words 'Maravan Catering'. Her flat was on the third floor of a middle-class 1920s house. Three high-ceilinged rooms, a conservatory, an old-fashioned bathroom, a loo with a cistern mounted almost at ceiling height, and a large kitchen with a new, free-standing dishwasher, whose outflow went into the sink.

It was the sort of flat you could only get with a large slice of luck and good contacts, and you always had the worry that the house might be sold and renovated, and the rent become unaffordable.

Until the break-up of her last relationship, Andrea had shared the flat with her partner, and now she felt a little lost in it. She lived in the bedroom and the kitchen. Sometimes in the conservatory, too. But she hardly ever used the sitting-cum-dining room, and she never went into Dagmar's bedroom, which had been emptied of everything.

Today, however, the sitting-cum-dining room was illuminated by a sea of candles. In the centre was Maravan's low table and his cushions. The tablecloth was his, too, and she had even wheedled out of him the domestic shrine with the goddess Lakshmi and the clay lamp. Maravan had succeeded in talking her out of the incense sticks and meditative Indian flute music.

They had brought over in Andrea's Golf all the kitchen equipment, cushions, table, ingredients and the dishes that he had had to pre-prepare at home.

He had visited her flat the day before to make and freeze the liquorice lollies. Likewise, he had brought along to put in the refrigerator the crunchy and chewy urad-strip construction, which he had spontaneously named 'man and woman'.

Everything else – the saffron and almond spheres, half-frozen in liquid nitrogen, the ghee cylinders threaded with saffron, the very glossy balls of ghee, long pepper, cardamom, cinnamon and palm sugar – he made in Andrea's kitchen. Even the sweetmeats to accompany the tea – the little red glazed hearts and the jellied asparagus – were served fresh. He also had to make his *modhakam*. Today Andrea had taken care of the delivery to the temple; he did not want the courier to come to her flat.

The rotary evaporator had been turning since ten o'clock that morning. After much searching Andrea had obtained it not through one of her catering contacts, but had borrowed it from a female admirer, a university assistant who was working on her chemistry dissertation.

Maravan had resisted the temptation to tinker with the three normal curry dishes, even though these were the only non-aphrodisiac recipes. Maybe the combination of these dishes with everything else had been responsible for the effect Andrea had experienced.

Andrea's guest arrived at eight o'clock. She was a very blonde, very nervous, slightly chubby, twenty-one-year-old, more pretty than beautiful. It was apparent that she did not feel at ease with the situation. She declined the champagne that Maravan served in his sarong and white shirt. He noted this deviation from the menu with some concern and hoped that it was not this particular ingredient which had hastened the effect.

When the two women had sat down, he brought his greeting from the kitchen, the mini chapattis, which he drizzled ceremoniously with his essence of curry leaves, cinnamon and coconut oil.

After that he served dishes only when Andrea rang a brass temple bell, another item borrowed from Maravan.

Each time the bell pealed and he brought in a new dish, Andrea's guest was more relaxed and, as a consequence, so was he. After serving the tea and sweetmeats, he bid goodbye with a short bow, as arranged.

He discreetly left the flat just before ten o'clock. Andrea would call him the next day and tell him when he should come past, so they could clear up and bring the stuff back to his place.

It was a muggy evening and in the sky he could still see the afterglow of the sun which had set a while ago. During the day the temperature had climbed above thirty degrees.

It was on these sorts of evenings that he felt most homesick. They reminded him of Colombo in the monsoon season. The first drops might fall at any moment, and sometimes he thought he could hear the distant surf of Galle Face Green, and the squawking of the ravens which stalked the food stalls on the promenade.

Even the smell could be similar just before the rain on muggy days, especially when the aroma of barbecues wafted in the air. Then he could smell them – the food stalls – and thought he could make out their lights twinkling in the distance.

But his homesickness was not so acute that evening. Today he felt that he had taken a step forwards. He had completed his first proper assignment as a hired chef in a Swiss home. No, hold on. Had he not supplied the furnishings and decoration? And had he not also served everything on his own? In fact, this evening had been Maravan Catering's first commission.

He was not tortured by lovesickness, either. Had Andrea been planning to spend the night with a man, he would surely have felt differently. But he was not envious of the blonde. If he were honest, it excited him to be complicit in her seduction. It made him feel a little closer to Andrea.

The heavens opened without any warning. He stopped, stretched out his arms and lifted his face to the rain. Like the young man he had watched from the tram some months back. Or like himself, as a boy in the first rain of the monsoon.

August 2008

13

If Huwyler's restaurant was not exactly full, he was busier than most of his rivals. Of course he could not help but know this; as the acting president of *swisschefs* he had all the figures at his fingertips. He was doing his best to resist the financial crisis, coming up with new ideas – the local press had written short, funny articles about his *Menu Surcrise*, for example – and now this had to happen!

That arsehole was having a heart attack on him. A full house on a Friday evening! Throwing up all over the table! And over the shirt front of his guest, a Dutch businessman.

Everyone must have been thinking: someone's dying before my very eyes in the Huwyler. What on earth has he eaten?

In an instant three doctors were attending to the patient, practically undressing the poor man. One of them gave a preliminary diagnosis – 'suspected myocardial infarction' – to the emergency services on his mobile, the second tried to revive him, while the third dashed outside, came back immediately with a bag and gave the man an injection. Ambulance sirens were already audible.

The paramedics and emergency doctor came in with a stretcher on wheels. Three tables had to be moved out of the way. Then they took him out, not a pretty sight: Dalmann, snow-white, oxygen mask, vomit sticking to his hair.

Of course the whole restaurant was in chaos after that. Dishes that had been called had to be taken back into the kitchen, half-eaten courses remained on tables, some diners wanted to pay, others were waiting for their tables to be put back in place, others felt sick. The wife of a well-known business lawyer was in hysterics. And everybody watched in disgust as the two Tamils cleared Dalmann's table and cleaned the floor.

Then came the *chef de service* with an air freshener – God knows where he got it from – and before Huwlyer could intervene the room no longer smelled of sick, but of pine needles and sick.

And finally, when Huwyler gave a short speech, which managed to appease those diners who had not vanished – he was confident that, thanks to the fortunate circumstance, albeit not unusual for his restaurant, that three doctors had been on hand immediately, the prognosis for the customer in question was very good – at the very moment when a semblance of normality had returned, Dalmann's guest came back from the staff changing room – freshly showered and wearing the sommelier's too-tight and too-short spare black suit – and actually asked to sit down and continue with his dinner! This, he emphasized with a raised voice, was exactly what his host would have wanted. Not surprisingly, his announcement ruined the appetite of a few more diners.

The following morning, when Huwyler called Schaeffer – Dalmann's colleague, who always made the bookings – to enquire about his boss's health, the man replied, 'As might be expected given the circumstances. Following emergency surgery the patient is in a stable condition.' He spoke like a medical bulletin.

There was one blessing: if Dalmann had died in the Huwyler it would have been more damaging to the business. On the other hand, the media might have reported it.

14

Andrea did not get in touch until the following afternoon.

Maravan was preparing the *modhakam* for the evening when the telephone rang. She sounded happy, but did not say whether the experiment had been a success. Maravan reined in his curiosity and did not ask.

Even when he was clearing up her kitchen an hour later he left it up to her. She watched him, a glass of water in her right hand, her elbow supported by the palm of her left. She made no move to help him.

'Aren't you at all curious?' she asked eventually.

'Yes,' was all he replied.

She put the glass on the kitchen table, took his shoulders in her hands, and kissed him on the forehead. 'You're a magician. It worked!'

The look he gave her must have been one of disbelief, because she repeated, a little more loudly this time, 'It worked!'

When he still did not react, she started skipping around him. 'Worked, worked, worked!' she said.

Only now did he laugh, temporarily joining in with her dance.

She shocked him with the description of her night of passion. Although she did not go into detail, she told him more than was appropriate to the moral sensitivities of a faithful Hindu. She finished off with the question: 'And do you know when she left?'

He cleared his throat: 'Judging by your tone I imagine it must have been late.'

'Half past two – this afternoon! Two-thirty.' She shot him a look of triumph.

'And why do you think the food was responsible? It could have been down to you as well.'

Andrea shook her head emphatically. 'Franziska doesn't sleep with women, Maravan. Never!'

She helped him load the equipment into her Golf and drove him home. For a brief half-hour he was able to imagine that part of his dream had come true: he and his partner Andrea ferrying the catering equipment back to the firm's headquarters after a successful job. He was pleased that she was lost in her thoughts, too, and did not break the spell of his reverie with conversation.

After everything had been put away in his flat, she made no move to leave. They stood on the tiny kitchen balcony, Andrea leaning against the railings with a cigarette. She did not inhale the smoke, and hastily stubbed it out soon afterwards, as if she were trying to nullify the drags she had taken. It had become noticeably cooler, but the rain had stopped a few hours earlier. From open windows came the music, chit-chat and laughter of Maravan's Tamil neighbours.

Down in the inner courtyard a dealer was concluding a rapid, silent transaction. Then both parties vanished.

'What's your greatest dream?' Andrea asked.

'Going back home, and peace.'

'No restaurant?'

'Sure. But in Colombo.'

'Until then?'

Maravan straightened himself, thrusting his hands into his trouser pockets. 'A restaurant here.'

'And how are you going to finance that?'

He shrugged. 'Catering?'

Andrea looked up at him. 'Exactly.'

He looked amazed. 'Do you think it might work?'

'If you cook as you did for me.'

Maravan laughed weakly. 'I see. What about the customers?'

'I'll worry about them.'

'And what do you get out of it?'

'Half.'

Andrea had a business plan and a little money. Eighteen months previously one of her mother's sisters had died childless, and had passed her inheritance to her four nieces and nephews. Apart from some savings, the legacy was a chalet with a few holiday apartments in a winter spa town in the Alpine foothills, where snow was not guaranteed and where the woman had spent half her life. The beneficiaries did not hesitate to sell the chalet. After deductions, each of them had received about 80,000 francs, of which Andrea only had about half left, because of her frequent changes of jobs. She wanted to invest some of it in Love Food, as she was now calling the company.

She would obtain the equipment Maravan needed – in particular the rotary evaporator. She would buy a stock of cutlery and crockery. She would take care of drumming up custom. She would swap her Golf for an estate. She would be responsible for the administration and service side and put up the initial business capital.

Maravan would provide the know-how.

Seen like that, Maravan had to admit that fifty-fifty was more than fair.

A *Love Dinner* for two would cost 1,000 francs, plus drinks, primarily champagne on the advice of the maestro, which they would be able to purchase wholesale and sell at restaurant prices.

Maravan was in agreement with everything. It may not have been the sort of catering he had envisaged, but in his culture there was nothing objectionable about the idea of dinners to enhance the love lives of married couples – Andrea's imagined clientele. And the prospect of spending a lot of time with Andrea made him happy.

'Why are you so keen on this?' he asked. 'You'd find another job easily.'

'It's something new,' she replied.

A rocket soared above the roofs, slowing down by the second, stopped for a moment, then plummeted back to earth in red strands that burnt themselves out. People were celebrating the first of August. And the founding of Love Food.

15

This was the second time that Maravan had cooked in Andrea's flat, but they had already developed a sort of routine. He knew where to find everything, and she no longer had to ask any questions when laying the table and decorating the room. They went about their work like a real team.

The guest that evening was Esther Dubois, a psychologist Andrea had met in a club some time back. She had been there with her husband, although this had not prevented her from making blatant advances towards Andrea.

Esther Dubois was a renowned sex therapist, who for a number of years wrote a well-regarded advice column in a magazine for women over forty. She was over forty too, had dyed her prematurely greying hair flaming red, and was a regular in the society pages.

Andrea had contacted her at her practice and had little trouble in persuading her to come. 'To an exciting culinary-sexual therapeutic experiment,' as she had put it.

She arrived half an hour late with a fat bunch of white arum lilies, because they suited the theme of the evening so well, she said. Andrea introduced Maravan with the following words, 'This is Sri Maravan, a great guru of erotic cuisine.'

She had not cleared the 'Sri' or the 'guru' with Maravan beforehand, and from his reaction she concluded that maybe she should have done. He held out his hand to the guest with a shy smile, then returned to his work.

'How exciting!' Esther Dubois said as Andrea showed her into the darkened room bathed in candlelight. She immediately made herself comfortable on the cushions and asked, 'No incense? No music?'

'Sri Maravan believes that both of these are distractions. One from the aroma of the food, the other from the pounding of the heart.' This line had not been cleared with him either. She took the temple bell and rang it. 'This is all he allows me.'

The door opened: Maravan brought in a tray with two champagne glasses and two small plates of mini chapattis. While the two women clinked glasses, he drizzled the curry leaf, cinnamon and coconut oil essence on to the small chapattis.

'No chemistry, I hope,' Esther Dubois remarked.

'Cooking is both chemistry and physics,' Maravan replied politely.

She took the chapatti, sniffed it, closed her eyes, bit off a piece, chewed solemnly, and popped her eyes open again. 'An incomparable piece of chemistry and physics.'

The therapist, normally a chatty woman, hardly said a word during the entire dinner. She restricted herself to making all sorts of sighing and moaning sounds, rolling her eyes and fanning herself theatrically. At one point she said, 'Do you know what the sexiest thing about this is? Eating with your hands.'

And when she had polished off the last of the glazed hearts with a contented sigh, she asked, 'What now? Your handsome guru?'

But the handsome guru had already gone.

*

This third dinner had the same effect on Andrea. It was a wonderful evening and wonderful night, even though Esther Dubois as a person left her cold. She found her too intellectual and somewhat too broad-minded. Andrea did not like these bi women in open relationships with their husbands, who could ring up around midnight and say, 'I'm not coming back tonight, hon. I'll tell you everything tomorrow.'

Anyway, the following morning she was happy that Esther had got up so early and had made a dash for it before breakfast, like an unfaithful husband.

'You'll be hearing from me,' Esther said when she came back into the bedroom and kissed her on the forehead. The promise was in reference to a short business chat during their night of passion. Andrea was pretty sure that she would keep to it.

'Does it always work?' Esther had asked with a sleepy voice.

'It does with me. Even with a man once!'

'I didn't know you slept with men too.'

'Me neither.'

'Extraordinary. What does he put in it?'

'They're ancient Ayurvedic aphrodisiac recipes. But he cooks them in his own very particular way.'

'Do you know how many of my patients would give their right arm for a meal like that?'

'Send them over,' was all Andrea replied, snuggling up in the duvet and finally going to sleep.

16

Dalmann was convinced that Schaeffer was trying to expose him to ridicule. The tracksuit he had brought him was red with neon-yellow arms. 'Couldn't you find anything more conspicuous?' he asked.

'I'm told that the more expressive colours are preferable at this time of year. Not least for safety considerations.'

'Who told you that?'

'I took some expert advice,' his colleague said, rather piqued.

Dalmann had put on the outfit, but in all honesty he did not care for it. None of the others looked any better in theirs, which were either too tight or too big. Nor did he care for the way they tried to atone for the sins of previous decades: slaves to their fitness machines, bright red in the face and out of breath.

Dalmann was sitting on an ergometer, pedalling without much effort. In a slot in front of the handlebars was a sheet of paper detailing his personal fitness programme. He was skipping the other exercises, concentrating instead on the ergometer. This allowed him to regulate his exertions and sit down at the same time. The doctor at the health farm had told him to do the exercises every day, but never push it to the limit. Dalmann had strictly observed the latter piece of advice.

They had inserted a stent, a tiny tube which expanded the constricted heart vessel that had been responsible for the infarction. It had not been a particularly invasive procedure; he had come through it well and now just had to complete this tiresome health farm treatment and take some medicine to regulate his blood clotting so that the tube stayed open. Apart from that he was supposed to lead a healthier lifestyle, watch what he ate and drank, and – the thing he found most difficult of all – give up smoking.

In the past he had always said, 'I'd rather be dead than go to a health farm.' Now, however, he did not find it so awful. It was like a luxury hotel with a slightly more professional wellness centre. Admittedly, the guests were older and more delicate, and the only thing they talked about was their health. But he did not have to talk to them, did he? Every other day Schaeffer came with his briefcase and they spent a few hours working in Dalmann's suite.

His pulse had risen above ninety. Dalmann again lowered his leisurely pedalling rate a touch, then a touch more, finally stopping altogether and getting off.

In the changing room he put on the white dressing gown with the large hotel logo embroidered on the chest, went to the kiosk, bought the most important papers, and shuffled towards the lift which took him to his floor.

The newspapers carried stories about the resignation of Pervez Musharraf. Dalmann wondered what effect that would have on his Pakistani connection.

He was going to have a shower, put on some normal clothes and allow himself a cigarette on the balcony. His non-smoking suite was full of no smoking signs.

But when he came back into the living room it was so dark he had to turn on the lights. Low-lying storm clouds had turned the gloomy summer's day into night. Dalmann opened the balcony door. The rain that sprayed in from the balcony darkened the light-beige fitted carpet.

September 2008

17

National banks around the world were pumping billions into the financial markets to ensure liquidity. Ten large banks set up a fund of 70 billion dollars to prevent international panic on the stock markets. And Lehman Brothers, the fourth largest American investment bank, had become insolvent.

Perhaps not the best time to start a company, Andrea thought, after Esther Dubois had hung up.

She had kept to her word and only two days after the dinner had telephoned to book an appointment for a 'patient couple'. Andrea had said yes, but now doubts were starting to emerge. She sat in the conservatory, in the creaky rattan chair which she had picked up with Dagmar at a flea market and painted green, and lit a cigarette.

When she thought about it, her life seemed to be a long series of rash decisions. She was easily enthused and quickly bored. Education, career choice, relationships, jobs – all by chance, spontaneous and changeable. Was that what she really wanted? To invest a large proportion of the money she had left in a catering service providing erotic dinners, which could not even operate legitimately?

She had made enquiries. She fulfilled all the requirements to obtain the police authorization to run a catering firm. That would be sorted out within a month. But the hygiene legislation presented an almost insurmountable obstacle. They would never be able to satisfy the endless regulations concerning kitchens and equipment, neither in her kitchen nor in Maravan's, no matter how squeaky clean they were. Even if they could meet the standards, the sites would have to be visited and checked by the commercial arm of the police, the building inspection department, the food inspection authority and fire service. On top of this, as an asylum seeker Maravan was not allowed to undertake any freelance work. She could not employ him as a chef either, only as a kitchen help – provided she got the authorization from the office for employment – and would have to pass herself off as the chef. It was all too complicated for a project which might fail. And who would pay back her investment if she could not obtain a licence? If she really wanted to see whether it would work in practice there was only one option: she would have to do it unofficially. At least to begin with.

But she did not need any of this. A week after her summary dismissal from the Huwyler she had already found another job. Not as stylish and gastronomic perhaps, but the pay was no worse and it had a younger, nicer clientele. It was called Mastroianni, an Italian restaurant right in the middle of the city's club scene. Even if she resigned from there – which she was planning to do because she found the hours too late – she would quickly find something else.

She stubbed out her half-smoked cigarette and pulled down the blinds of the west-facing window. It was a warm summer's day and the afternoon sun would otherwise soon heat up the conservatory. The light filtering through the faded brown material gave the room an old-fashioned feel with its cobbled-together furniture and two dusty indoor palms. Andrea sat back down and indulged in the fantasy that she was part of an old yellowed photograph.

Maybe it would have been better to keep her distance from Maravan after she had discovered his secret. That evening with him had preyed on her mind. She had needed to know for certain that it really had all been down to the food.

But what about the convincing result of the experiment with Franziska, who had been uncontactable since that night? Was that not proof enough for her? Even so, it was no reason to question her whole existence and personality. And certainly no reason to share her work and future with the very man who had laid a trap for her. Even though she did not hold it against him, it was something that would always stand between them.

She took a cigarette out of the packet with its bold death warning. When Dagmar still lived here, smoking was prohibited throughout the flat. The two of them had given up together. But after they split up, Andrea had started again and allowed herself to smoke in the conservatory. She did not have a garden, after all.

The cultural differences between her and Maravan would soon lead to problems, too. The 'Sri' and 'guru' had already caused a slight upset. 'Please don't introduce me as Sri and guru,' he had said politely but firmly. 'If my people knew that I was letting myself be called those things I would be finished.'

No, it was a bad idea, whichever way you looked at it.

She put her cigarette in the ashtray and watched the smoke rise in a thin, vertical line until it was disturbed by the fronds of a palm leaf.

Maybe it was this image which inspired her to do it after all.

Oh, just this once, she thought, they could give it a go.

The shutters were closed in Maravan's sitting room, but all doors and windows were open to allow a slight draught. Wearing only a sarong, Maravan was sitting in the half darkness in front of his screen, reading the news from his native country.

The Sri Lankan government had ordered all United Nations and other aid organizations to leave the northern provinces by the end of the month. Almost one quarter of a million Tamils were on the run. A humanitarian crisis was waiting to happen.

A few of the Liberation Tigers' planes had attacked the air base and police headquarters in Vavuniya, a district which the Sri Lankan government had declared liberated a long time ago. With the help of the artillery, the Tigers had destroyed the radar system, anti-aircraft guns and the munitions depot, and killed countless soldiers.

In retaliation the Sri Lankan army was bombarding the A9 highway and the surrounding villages in the Mu'rika'ndi district. Traffic had been paralysed on the A9 in the direction of the

Oamanthai checkpoint. Relief supplies and medicines were no longer getting past the checkpoints.

This meant that Maravan needed more money. Increasingly, his family had to buy on the black market, where prices rose every day. Especially for medicines.

On top of this, Ori the moneylender charged steep penalties for defaulting on interest payments and was merciless in exacting them. And the organizations close to the LTTE were doubling their contributions because – how often had this been claimed? – they were in a decisive stage of the war of liberation.

Maravan was still jobless and the little that he earned in addition to his unemployment benefit by making *modhakam* was nowhere near enough to cover all his debts.

He was in a pretty desperate situation, therefore, when Andrea called and told him about Love Food's first commission. He did not hesitate for a second.

His only question was: 'Are they married?'

'For thirty years,' Andrea replied, rather amused.

That was that as far as Maravan was concerned.

18

From the kitchen you could see the city, the lake and the hills opposite. Maravan was standing beside a snow-white kitchen island under a huge stainless-steel extractor fan which made nothing more than a quiet humming sound, like the air conditioning in a luxury hotel. The large dining table with twelve stackable chairs, also white, was not laid. The dinner was to be served in the sitting room next door, which was vast and full of art. It, too, had a glass front with a view of the roof terrace and a panorama of the city. With these sorts of dinners – Andrea called them *Love Menus* – the presence of the cook in the same room was naturally undesirable.

Maravan found the situation rather embarrassing, as clearly did the hostess, Frau Mellinger. She was closer to sixty than fifty, very soignée, and slightly stiff, maybe just today and because of the occasion. She kept finding excuses to enter the kitchen, where she would cover her eyes affectedly and call out, 'I'm not looking! I'm not looking!'

Herr Mellinger had retired to his study. He also seemed to find the whole thing awkward. He was a gaunt man in his sixties, with short-cropped white hair, dressed in black and wearing black-rimmed spectacles. He had made a brief appearance, greeting Maravan with an embarrassed cough. When Andrea entered the kitchen immediately afterwards, his disgruntled expression brightened. Then he apologized and muttered, 'I'll leave you now to do your magic.'

Only Andrea felt no embarrassment about the affair. She moved around this gigantic penthouse totally naturally, as if it were her own, and wore her golden-yellow sari with total self-assurance. Although Maravan always thought there was something not quite right about European women in saris, they somehow looked authentic on Andrea with her long, shiny, black hair, despite her snow-white complexion.

The menu was the tried and trusted one:

Mini chapattis with essence of curry leaf, cardamom and coconut oil
Urad lentil ribbons in two consistencies
Ladies' fingers curry on sali rice with garlic foam
Poussin curry on sashtika rice with coriander foam
Churaa varai on nivara rice with mint foam
Frozen saffron and almond foam with saffron textures
Sweet and spicy spheres of cardamom, cinnamon and ghee
Glazed chickpea, ginger and pepper vulvas
Jellied asparagus and ghee phalluses
Liquorice, honey and ghee ice lollies

Andrea had persuaded him to introduce a couple of creative innovations. She suggested they serve the asparagus-and-ghee jellies in the form of penises, rather than asparagus spears. And the glazed hearts became pussies, as she called them. Maravan thought this was too explicit and had made a fuss. But Andrea said, 'I've seen pictures of erotic frescoes which your ancestors painted on the Sigiriya rock fifteen hundred years ago. So don't play the prude with me.'

Maravan gave in. But in shame he covered his sweetmeats with baking paper, in case Frau Mellinger unexpectedly popped into the kitchen again.

If Love Food were to have an official company logo, Andrea thought it would have to be a temple bell. She was sitting with Maravan in the kitchen, listening out for the ring from the room where the Mellingers were giving their relationship a fresh impetus. She kept on thinking she had heard something, rushed out to listen at the door, and came back empty-handed.

'What are we going to do if it doesn't work?' Maravan asked.

'It will work,' Andrea replied determinedly. 'And even if it doesn't, we wouldn't find out. Nobody's going to admit that they've spent well over a thousand francs on an erotically stimulating dinner that hasn't worked.'

When she had served the champagne and appetizers, she came back giggling. 'She's wrapped up in flowing cloths, see-through ones,' she reported.

After the lentil ribbons she told him, 'I presented the starters as "man and woman", and he asked, "Which one's the man, the soft or hard one?"'

Embarrassed, Maravan said nothing.

'Of course, I said, "Both."' Andrea paused for effect. 'And she said, "I hope so."'

The gaps between the courses became longer. From time to time Andrea went onto the roof terrace for a cigarette. It was dark now, the lights of the city were reflected in the lake, the suburbs sprinkled the hills with dots of light.

After the main course the temple bell remained silent. Maravan was getting nervous. The next course was the trickiest as far as timing was concerned. He had to cook the spheres for five minutes in algin water, rinse them with cold water, inject them with ghee, and then put them in the oven for about twenty minutes at sixty degrees. He could not allow half an hour to pass before dessert, and so ten minutes after Andrea had served the curries he had made the spheres, cooked them, injected them with ghee and rinsed them in cold water. He was afraid that they might collapse if they did not go in the oven soon.

'Please go and check,' he now asked her a second time.

She went out, wondering whether she should knock or clear her throat. But halfway to the door she heard noises coming from the room that made the decision for her.

She returned to the kitchen and said, 'Job done. I think they'll pass on dessert.'

After this first job Andrea's doubts had evaporated. The feedback the Mellingers gave their therapist was so positive that already the next day Esther Dubois was holding out the prospect of further bookings. The net income after deducting the raw materials and the cost price of the champagne was almost 1,400 francs. The work was easy, she did not have to put up with a boss, and Maravan was a quiet, polite and unassuming work colleague.

But what tipped the scales was that Love Food had been her idea. It could not have happened had she not come up with the notion of using the Tamil asylum-seeker's culinary arts of seduction for the purposes of sexual therapy. And you also had to have the right contacts to market such an idea.

One of the things about her career that had bored Andrea was the lack of creativity. She had endless ideas, but never the opportunity to put them into practice. With Love Food this had changed radically. The idea was her baby, she was proud of it. And if it also brought in money, then she saw no reason why she should give it up.

Soon afterwards, when Esther Dubois requested a booking for another couple, she said yes immediately. Maravan had no reservations either. Apart from the question: 'Are they married?'

Most clients were couples over the age of forty from income groups that allowed for the existence of such problems, as well as the therapy to treat them. All at once Maravan gained an insight into a layer of society he had never been in contact with before, apart from at a great distance as a chef at luxury hotels in southern India and Sri Lanka. He entered houses in which the cost of a chair or a tap could have met the financial needs of his relatives back home for many months.

He moved around their kitchens like a member of the household, even though he felt like a blind passenger in an alien spaceship.

Maravan had believed that, with every year he spent in this country, the mentality and culture of its inhabitants was becoming more familiar. But now he had glimpsed behind the scenes, he realized just how foreign these people and their problems were. The way they spoke, the way they lived, the way they dressed, what they considered important – he found all of this strange.

He would rather have kept his distance. It troubled him that he was forced to intrude into the intimacy of these people. In the past he had found it disturbing enough that they did not seem to think it was important to keep their private lives private. They kissed in public, on the tram they spoke about the most personal things, schoolgirls dressed like prostitutes, and in the papers, on the television, in the cinema, in music, it was all about sex.

He did not want to know, see or hear any of that. Not because he was a prude. Where he came from they venerated the female as the fundamental power of the world. His gods had penises and his goddesses had breasts and vaginas. The mothers of his gods were not virgins. No, he did not have a troubled relationship with sexuality. It played an important role in his culture, religion and medicine. But here he found it embarrassing. And he also guessed why: because in spite of the fact that it was everywhere, deep down these people found it embarrassing.

But business was going well. Only four weeks after the Mellingers, Love Food had five bookings in a single week. A fortnight later they were fully booked for the first time.

At the end of September they shared a net profit of 17,000 francs. Tax-free.

October 2008

19

For Maravan, being fully booked meant that he spent the entire day and half of the night in the kitchen. At six in the morning he would begin preparing for the following day; shortly after midday Andrea would come by with the estate and they would start loading the thermoboxes and other kitchen equipment.

It was hard work and a little monotonous, because he had to cook exactly the same menu every time. But Maravan enjoyed the independence, the recognition and Andrea's company. Day by day they became closer, albeit not in the way he had hoped, unfortunately. They became colleagues who enjoyed working together, and perhaps they were well on the way to becoming friends.

One of those lunchtimes Andrea brought up a bundle of post that had been sticking out of his overflowing box. Among the flyers and brochures (multiple quantities of which had been stuffed through the slot to deliver their load more quickly) was an airmail letter addressed to Maravan in a child's hand. It came from his nephew Ulagu and ran:

Dear Uncle,

I hope you are well. We are not so well. Here there are many who fled to Jaffna before the war. Often there is not enough food for us all. People say we're going to lose the war, and they're worried about what will happen afterwards. But Nangay says it can't get any worse.

I'm writing this letter to you because of Nangay. She's in a very bad way, but does not want you to know. She's very thin, drinks only water all day long and does it in her bed every night. The doctor says she'll dehydrate if she doesn't get her medicine. He's written down for me what she's got and what the medicine's called. Maybe you can get it there and send it to us. I don't want Nangay to dehydrate.

I send you my best wishes and thanks. I hope that the war's over soon and you can come back. Or I'll come to you and work as a chef. I can already cook quite well.

Your nephew,

Ulagu

Ulagu was the eldest son of Maravan's youngest sister Ragini. He was eleven when Maravan left the country and he was the person Maravan had found it most difficult to say goodbye to. Maravan had been just like Ulagu when he was a boy – quiet, dreamy and slightly secretive. And like Maravan he wanted to be a chef and spent a lot of time with Nangay in the kitchen.

Because of Ulagu, Maravan sometimes felt that he had left a part of himself behind. Thanks to Ulagu it was still there.

'Bad news?' Andrea had watched him read the letter while she carried out the equipment on to the landing.

Maravan nodded. 'My nephew says that my grandmother's in a very bad way.'

'The cook?'

'Yes.'

'What's wrong with her?'

Maravan read from the note enclosed with the letter: 'Diabetes insipidus.'

'My grandmother's had diabetes for years,' Andrea said to console him. 'You can live with it till you're ancient.'

'It isn't really diabetes, it's just called that. You drink the whole time, but you can't retain the water and over time you dehydrate.'

'Can it be treated?'

'It can. But they can't get the medicine.'

'Well, you must get hold of it here, then.'

'I will.'

The waiting room was small and overcrowded. Almost all the patients were asylum seekers. Most were Tamils, though there was a handful of Eritreans and Iraqis. Over the last few years Dr Kerner had become *the* doctor for refugees, more by chance than intention. It had all started when he employed a Tamil assistant. The word had soon got around the Tamil diaspora that Tamil was spoken at Dr Kerner's. The first Africans came later, and now the Iraqis as well.

Maravan had waited an hour before getting a seat. Now there were only four more patients in front of him.

He had come in the hope of obtaining a prescription. Maybe he would be able to send Nangay the medicine. Although it was getting more and more difficult, there were still ways. He would have to rely on the services of the LTTE, but he could accept that. After all, Nangay's life was at stake.

The last patient before Maravan was called in, an elderly Tamil lady. She stood up, bowed with her hands together before the image of Shiva on the wall, and followed the assistant.

On the wall of Dr Kerner's waiting room Shiva, the Buddha, a crucifix and a hand-written verse from the Koran hung side by side peacefully. Not every patient was happy with this arrangement, but as far as the doctor was concerned they could stay away if they didn't like it.

A long time passed before Maravan could hear the assistant saying goodbye to the woman, offering a few comforting words. Just before six o'clock he was led into the consulting room.

Dr Kerner could have been around fifty. He had unruly white hair and tired eyes set in a youthful face. He wore an open doctor's coat and a stethoscope, more to inspire confidence than out of necessity. When Maravan came in, he looked up from his patient file, pointed to the chair by his desk and continued reading the patient history. Maravan had been to see him some time ago because of a burn he had suffered while handling a frying pan in a professional kitchen.

'It's not about me,' Maravan explained when the assistant had left. 'It's about my grandmother in Jaffna.'

He told the doctor about Nangay's illness and the difficulty of obtaining the medicine.

Dr Kerner listened, nodding all the while as if he had heard the story long ago. 'And now you want a prescription,' he said before Maravan had even finished.

He nodded.

'Are your great aunt's circulation, blood pressure and coronary arteries all OK?'

'She has a strong heart,' Maravan said. '"If only my heart weren't so strong," she always says, "I'd have stopped being a burden to you long ago."'

Dr Kerner took his prescription pad. While he was writing, he said, 'It's an expensive medicine.' He tore off the sheet and pushed it across his desk. 'A repeat prescription for a year. How are you going to get the medicine to your great aunt?'

'By courier to Colombo and from there . . .' – Maravan shrugged – 'somehow.'

Dr Kerner thought for a moment, his chin in his hand. 'An acquaintance of mine works for Médecins Sans Frontières. You know the Sri Lankan government has instructed all aid organizations to leave the north by the end of the month. She's flying to Colombo tomorrow morning to help the delegation with their move. I could ask her whether she'd take the medicine with her. What do you think?'

20

This was the time when Hindus were celebrating Navarathiri, the struggle of good against evil.

When the gods felt themselves powerless against the forces of evil, they each broke off a part of their divine power and used it to fashion another goddess: Kali. In a terrible battle lasting nine days and nights she defeated the demon Mahishasura.

When the anniversary of this battle comes around, Hindus pray for nine days to Saraswati, the goddess of learning, Lakshmi, the goddess of prosperity, and Kali, the goddess of power.

Maravan had bookings every day and evening during Navarathiri. The only thing he was capable of doing when he got home late and tired was to make his *puja* – the daily prayer before the domestic shrine – a little longer and more celebratory, and offer up to the goddesses some of the food he had put aside for them. At the very least he needed to thank Lakshmi for the fact that he had sufficient money to send a regular sum back home and hardly any more debts.

On the tenth day, however, he got his own way. On Vijayadasami, the night of victory, he went to the temple as he had done every year since he could remember.

He had brought it to Andrea's attention several weeks previously, and she had marked the date in her diary with a thick pen. But a few days later she had come to him and said casually, 'I had to take a booking on the day of that unpronounceable festival of yours. Is that awful?'

'On Vijayadasami?' he asked in disbelief.

'Otherwise they couldn't have done it for three weeks.'

'Then cancel again.'

'I can't do that now.'

'You'll have to do the cooking then.'

Andrea did cancel, and these fledgling business partners had their first argument.

It had rained heavily overnight. A filthy grey stratus of low cloud lay over the lowlands for the entire day. But it was almost twenty degrees, warm and dry. Singing, drumming and clapping hands behind the vehicle carrying the image of Kali, the procession moved across the car park by the industrial building, which was where the temple stood, and which had been cleared of cars for the occasion.

Maravan had joined the procession. In contrast to many other men who were in traditional dress, he wore a suit, white shirt and tie. Only the sign of blessing that the priest had painted on his forehead indicated that he was not a detached onlooker.

'Where's your wife?' a voice next to him asked. It was the young Tamil woman he had knocked over in the tram. She had raised her head and was giving him a searching look. What was her name? Sandana?

'Hello Sandana. *Vanakkam*, welcome. I don't have a wife.'

'But my mother saw her. In your flat.'

'When was your mother in my flat?'

'She came to fetch *modhakam* for the temple.'

Now he remembered. That was why he thought he had seen the woman before.

'Oh, that was Andrea. She's not my wife. We work together. I cook and she looks after the organization and service side.'

'She's not a Tamil.'

'No, she was born here.'

'So was I. But I'm still a Tamil.'

'I think she's Swiss. Why does it interest you?'

Her dark skin became a little darker. But she did not avert her gaze. 'I only have to look at you . . .'

The procession had reached the entrance to the temple. The crowd formed a semicircle around the statue of Kali. In the throng Maravan was pressed up against Sandana. She lost her balance for a split second and held on to him tightly. He could feel her warm hand on his wrist, which she held a little longer than necessary.

'Kali, Kali! Why won't you help us?' sobbed a woman. She thrust her hands out to the goddess in supplication and then slapped them in front of her face. Two women beside her took hold of her and led her away.

When Maravan turned back to Sandana he saw her mother dragging the girl away, while giving her a good talking to.

21

The financial crisis had hit Europe. Britain had nationalized Bradford & Bingley, the Benelux states had bought 49 per cent of the financial company Fortis. The Danish bank, Roskilde, was only able to survive thanks to its competitors. The Icelandic government had taken over the third-largest bank, Glitnir, and shortly afterwards had put all banks under state control and issued urgent warnings that the country was in danger of going bankrupt.

European governments made 1 trillion euros available to the financial sector.

The Swiss government also announced that, if necessary, it would take further measures to stabilize the financial system and safeguard the deposits of bank customers.

The crisis had not yet hit the Huwyler. Except in the person of Eric Dalmann.

He was sitting with his investment adviser, Fred Keller, at table one as usual, but this evening it was on his guest's bill. Not because things had got that bad, but because it was time Keller felt in his own wallet the damage he had caused.

For Keller had invested a substantial chunk of his venture capital – as Dalmann, with a wink, liked to call that portion of his money which he invested more speculatively – in the American subprime market. Dalmann did not reproach him for this; after all, Keller was an investor happy to take risks. What he did hold against Keller, however, was the fact that the latter had advised him to sit out the crisis when it was still in its infancy. The second crude blunder was that he had conducted all of this business via Lehman Brothers. The third, that the share of the capital which had been left in Europe had chiefly been invested in bonds in Icelandic krona.

And the fourth, that a considerable proportion of the non-speculative remainder of his fortune was in financial stocks – shares in the largest Swiss bank.

It had thus been a fairly silent meal up until now. They were eating the starter of the *Menu Surprise*, truffled quail mousse with essence of quail and apple crystals: Dalmann in his greedy, thoughtless fashion, Keller with a little more care and good manners.

'Nobody could have seen it coming,' he stressed. He had uttered this sentence once already, before the waiter had served the dish. But Dalmann had not reacted.

Now he did. 'So why's it so full in here, then?' he snapped. 'All this lot are perfectly relaxed. Who's been advising them?'

'Maybe they have a lower share of risk capital. It's the client who determines the proportion of risk capital. The client says what percentage of his capital he wants to invest conservatively and how much a bit more dynamically.'

'Dynamically!' Dalmann spluttered, catapulting a tiny piece of quail mousse onto the plate of his adviser. With a stony expression Keller looked at his starter, only half finished, and put down his knife and fork side by side on the plate.

Dalmann had emptied his plate and also put down his cutlery. 'So let's talk about conservative investments. UBS, for example.'

'But they were blue chips. Nobody –'

Dalmann interrupted him: 'Are they going down? Are they going up?'

'Up in the long term.'

'In the long term I'm going to be dead.'

At that moment Huwyler came to the table. Before he could open his mouth, Dalmann said, 'No real sign of the crisis in here, is there?'

'People always have to eat,' Huwyler replied. Not for the first time that evening.

'And quality knows no crisis,' Dalmann added.

'That's what I always say,' Huwyler said, grinning.

'I know. What's the next course?'

'A surprise. That's why the menu is called *Surprise*.'

'Oh come on, tell me. I've had enough surprises today already.'

Huwyler hesitated. 'Breton lobster,' he said.

'How's it done?'

'That's the surprise.'

'You don't know, do you?'

'Of course I do.'

'That's why you got rid of those cloches, so you can see what's being served.'

Huwyler took the opportunity to change the subject. 'Do you miss the cloches, then?'

'I thought that they enhanced the food.'

'And I thought it didn't need any enhancing.'

Huwyler was saved by the waiter who came to clear the plates.

It was not exactly a life and death scenario for Dalmann, but he still had some serious problems.

Many of his Russian business friends for whom he had brokered contacts and created an agreeable business climate here were feeling the crisis and staying away.

Then there was the Liechtenstein affair. German tax investigators had paid an informant for the bank details of hundreds of German nationals with accounts at the Landesbank. This not only had a negative impact on Dalmann's brokering contacts in Liechtenstein, but it also put pressure on bank secrecy in Switzerland and thus made life more difficult for his activities as intermediary and consultant.

And then the subject of destroying documents in the nuclear smuggling affair also kept on flaring up. Each time with the risk that the name Palucron and Dalmann's former role as a director there would appear in the press.

All this would have been more bearable without his health worries as well. Although he had made a good recovery since his heart attack, he was not the man he used to be. The incident had reminded him of his mortality and taken away some of his *joie de vivre*. Although he continued to do all the things that Anton

Hottinger, his friend and doctor, had always forbidden him, he now did them with a bad conscience. This was something that had never troubled him before, certainly not in relation to his lifestyle. He had once heard that the vices you indulged in with a bad conscience were far unhealthier than all the others.

This is why recently he had started working systematically on his conscience rather than his vices. Up until now it had not brought him any noticeable improvement.

22

Until recently Andrea had resisted taking over Dagmar's bedroom. She wanted to keep open the option of having a flatmate. But Love Food was now going so well that she could afford to live here alone. So now she was using the room as an office.

She had not found it easy to remove the last traces of Dagmar: the bits of Sellotape which had attached stills from her favourite films to the wall. Dagmar was a cinema freak. She loved difficult art-house movies in incomprehensible languages, owned a collection of Swedish silent movies, and was an expert on post-revolutionary Russian cinema. This passion had been the cause of many crises in their relationship. Not only because Andrea's taste in films was completely different, but mainly because their jobs allowed them so little time off together. Dagmar was a dental hygienist, and Andrea did not want to spend each one of the few free evenings she had with her girlfriend watching films about social issues.

But Dagmar's obsession was also part of the reason why Andrea was so fascinated with her. She dressed, made herself up and styled her hair like a silent film star, smoked with a long cigarette holder before they both gave up together, and arranged her bedroom like a star's dressing room from the 1920s. The fact that Andrea liked to look slightly glamorous was a vestige of her relationship with Dagmar.

Now the room had been freshly painted and furnished with office gear: a desk with PC and telephone, and an adjustable swivel chair. Everything apart from the telephone and computer came from a second-hand shop near Maravan's flat.

The only thing that still reminded her of Dagmar was a forgotten rock crystal prism, which hung from a long piece of string in front of one of the two windows, and occasionally refracted the rays of the morning sun into its spectral colours, scattering them into the room as colourful patches of light.

Andrea did not really need an office; a few telephone numbers, two files and a diary would have sufficed for the administrative side of Love Food. But it made the whole thing more professional. With an office, Love Food became a company and her job became a career.

Another reason for not keeping the room spare was that the few female visitors who stayed the night slept in her bed. She was living the life of a single woman and had no intention of entering into another serious relationship so soon. Love Food did not allow her any time to feel lonely.

She was sitting in this office, watching the colourful patches of light dance on the walls, when Herr Mellinger, her first ever customer, called. She was slightly surprised. Although quite a few couples booked Love Food a second time, until now everything had come via the practice of Esther Dubois, the therapist. It was a new thing for someone to contact her directly.

It was not long before Andrea discovered the reason.

Slightly embarrassed, Herr Mellinger cleared his throat and then came to the point: 'Do you also do, erm, discreet dinners?'

'If we weren't discreet we would have to shut up shop.'

'No sure, I mean, erm, discreet as far as Frau Doctor Dubois is concerned?'

'I'm not sure I understand.'

'I mean, do you also do those dinners without her knowledge?'

Andrea thought for a moment. Then she decided she would not recklessly jeopardize their business relationship with Esther, who took a 10 per cent cut. 'I don't think that would be fair. And it might compromise the success of the therapy.'

'Not as part of the therapy.' Now Mellinger sounded rather impatient.

And when Andrea still failed to understand, he became more specific: 'Not my wife. Do you understand?'

Andrea understood. But if Esther found out . . .

'I'll pay double.'

But then again, who would tell Esther? Certainly not Mellinger.

She therefore agreed and arranged a date.

The sitting room in the three-roomed maisonette was on the first floor, which was accessed via a spiral staircase. It was stuffed full of pink kitsch: cushions, dolls, cuddly toys, porcelain trinkets, pictures, blankets, wall hangings, feather boas, tutus, glitz, glimmer, fashion jewellery.

'I collect pink things,' Alina had explained when she showed

Andrea into the room. She was a short blonde woman, very sweet if you liked that type. And Mellinger obviously did. The flat certainly had not been cheap. It was new, in a good part of town, and the interior was expensive.

'Shall we stick to first names? You can't be that much older than me,' Alina said.

Andrea agreed. By her reckoning she was even a little younger.

'I'll let you get on. Please make yourselves at home,' Alina had said, absenting herself for the afternoon. 'I'd just get in your way.'

Andrea and Maravan dragged the round table, the cushions and the cloths up the spiral staircase. These were no longer Maravan's private possessions: Love Food had acquired them.

'Not really apt, I fear,' Andrea said to Maravan, pointing at all the pink.

'On the contrary: for us Hindus pink is the colour of the heart chakra. Green and pink. The centre of love, *kaadhal*.'

Andrea set about preparing the room, Maravan retired to the kitchen.

Later, while Andrea watched him intertwine the crunchy and elastic strips of urad lentils – something else he performed with greater craftsmanship each time – he said, shaking his head, more to himself than to her, 'It's strange, she's so young and yet she's got these problems already.'

Andrea had not filled him in about the particular circumstances of this job and its fee. She did not say anything now either, and, unless it became necessary, had no intention of doing so later.

*

He would never have known if it had not been for that spiral staircase.

Andrea was carrying the tray with the ghee spheres upstairs. Halfway up she trod on the hem of her sari. Rather than dropping the tray and holding on to the rail, she tried to regain her balance without using her hands and twisted her ankle.

She just about managed to serve the dish and hobble back into the kitchen. But then she sat on a chair and examined her ankle. It was already a bit swollen. Maravan had to fill in for her.

He carried the tray with the tea and sweetmeats up the stairs and knocked.

'Come in,' a man's voice called.

Maravan entered the room. The candlelight gave a golden gleam to the sea of pink. Alina was slumped back on the cushions. When she realized that it was not Andrea she covered her breasts with her arm and let out an 'Oh!' which was more amused than shocked.

The man was sitting with his back to the door. Now he turned his head and said, 'Hee, hee.' He was naked to the waist as well.

Maravan recognized him. It was Herr Mellinger, the first Love Food client. He wondered for a moment whether he ought to go out again and give the two of them the opportunity to put on a few clothes.

'Don't mind us,' Alina said. 'We're feeling pretty hot already.'

Maravan put the tray onto the table and cleared away the crockery from the previous course. He tried not to look at either of them, but he could not ignore a pair of men's trousers and some pink lingerie which were strewn beside the table.

'Why didn't you say anything?' he asked Andrea in the kitchen.

'This time you didn't ask if they were married.'

'Because I thought I could take that for granted.'

'Why's it so important?'

'If they're married, this is perfectly normal. Now it's something else. Now it's improper.'

Andrea looked as if she was struggling to come to a decision. Then she said, 'That's why it's better paid. Like all improper things.'

November 2008

23

Barack Obama had won the election at a canter. From next year, the United States would be governed for the first time in its history by a black president. The world marvelled and Europe applauded, almost more enthusiastically than the country which had elected him.

It was only those in Dalmann's circles, both national and international, who were sceptical. They had feared the Democrats might win, as they had worried during the previous two elections as well. They found the Republicans' economic, foreign and in particular their fiscal policy more predictable and compatible.

'Bad news,' was Dalmann's reply when Schaeffer woke him with confirmation of what had been looming the night before: the European economy had now officially slipped into recession. The GDP of the Eurozone had fallen for the second quarter in succession.

For Dalmann this was the signal to turn his attention again to those business areas from which he had been gradually distancing himself in the last few years.

In the bar of the Imperial Hotel four men were sitting having drinks. The pianist was playing golden oldies, discreetly, but loud enough to allow private conversations to take place at the tables.

The men had eaten and drunk well at the Huwyler and were now allowing themselves a nightcap. Until the women arrived.

Four inconspicuous figures in dark suits: two Europeans, one American and an Asian. The last of these was about fifty and wore large, round glasses. As was the custom in Thailand, everybody called him by his nickname. His was Waen: glasses.

They talked in English, one with a Thai accent, two with Swiss twangs, and one with a drawl from the southern states.

The American's name was Steven X. Carlisle. Steve owned a small import-export firm in Memphis. Besides other things, he was an intermediary for the buying and selling of new and used products from his country's armouries. Waen's company, which had its headquarters in Bangkok, also worked in this field.

The two other men were Eric Dalmann and Hermann Schaeffer, his colleague.

This was the first time that Steve and Waen had met. Dalmann had arranged the meeting and the two of them had hit it off instantly. Before dinner they had done some serious work in Dalmann's office and all were happy with the result.

It was a deal which Dalmann would have left well alone if times had been better. But given the financial crisis – his personal one, too – and the fact that the deal was *almost* legal, Dalmann had agreed to take on the role of intermediary.

The goods were non-upgraded armoured howitzers from the 1950s that had been rejected by the Swiss army and were destined for scrap. Waen could find buyers for the equipment; the only problem was Swiss legislation. It did permit the export of these goods to Thailand, but only if a declaration was signed that they would not be exported again to a third country, something the Swiss would be able to monitor.

The risk that the controls would actually be carried out was not high, but it was an ever-present one, given domestic political sensitivities. Arms exports to countries at war was currently a hot topic, and a referendum to ban such exports was in the offing.

Several years ago, however, the Government had made a decision on the export of munitions which solved this problem. Disused munitions could be returned to their country of manufacture without the need for a declaration that they would not be re-exported. In the case of the M109 armoured howitzers, this country was the United States of America.

This is where Steve came in. He would buy the goods for the manufacturer at a notional price and supply them to Waen as products of the country where they were made. This would not be a problem as the United States was the largest arms supplier to Thailand.

Schaeffer had arranged a meeting for the following afternoon between Carlisle, Dalmann and the official responsible for writing off the howitzers. With a lunch to follow.

Waen would join them when the official had left.

The barman brought two long-legged women in cocktail dresses to the table. The taller of them was black. Her short-cropped hair looked like the tight-fitting cap of an Olympic swimmer. The four men stood to welcome them. Two of them gave the women their chairs and bade the others farewell until the following day.

24

It was only a telephone call, but it had grave consequences. Andrea was shopping in the household section of a department store. She was choosing cloths, cushions, candlesticks and a few other decorative items. Not because Love Food urgently needed them, but simply because it was Indian Week at the shop and business was good.

Her mobile rang and the display said it was Esther, the therapist.

'Hi Esther!' Andrea said, exaggerating her delight. '*So* nice to hear from you!'

Esther was abrupt and came straight to the point. 'It's my job to solve couple's problems, not create them. And so I'm ending our business relationship forthwith.'

'I don't understand.' Andrea's voice had become serious and soft.

'Mellinger's wife found out about his affair. He mentioned you. How could you?'

'He wouldn't take no for an answer. I'm really sorry.'

'Me too.'

That is when Esther terminated the conversation. Andrea put back the things she had chosen. Although Love Food had a good number of bookings for the next fortnight, there were no other reservations after that.

Esther had meant it seriously. Andrea tried to get her to change her mind, but to no avail. 'You know what?' Esther had said. 'I've got my reputation to think of. If Love Food is going to be that underhand, I might as well send my patients straight to a brothel.'

Andrea had suspected that Esther was happy to have an excuse to end their relationship, and she made the mistake of telling her so. 'Sure,' she remarked, 'if your patients come directly to us rather than to you, you'll be left with nothing.'

Had there been the slightest chance of making Esther change her mind, Andrea had blown it with this comment.

She did not inform Maravan of this development immediately. It was he who finally asked, 'Have we had fewer enquiries or are you not accepting them all any more?'

Only then did she make her confession.

He listened calmly, then said, 'So I can finally cook something else again.'

'And where am I going to get the customers for normal dinners?'

'My dinners are never normal,' Maravan answered.

Andrea was right. Without the erotic element, Love Food was merely another small catering firm, with the handicap that it was operating illegally and dependent on word of mouth for business. But who would put the word around for a firm that nobody knew about? They needed a way in.

Andrea tried in vain to get their first commission. It was Maravan who had the obvious idea: 'Why don't you just invite people over? And if they like it you can tell them that we can also do it at their homes.'

She put together a list of those people she knew who were most active socially, most comfortable financially, most willing to experiment and most communicative, and came up with twelve names. Not a single man among them.

They set a date for 15 November. In Washington, the twenty leading industrial and emerging nations met at a global finance summit and decided on a reorganization of the world's financial markets. The Sri Lankan army continued to shell the city of Kilinochchi. And the Swiss Defence Minister was bullied out of his post by his own party.

Andrea was decorating the dining room and setting the table. They had decided to use cutlery and not eat on the floor. Maravan had even allowed her to play some Indian background music. He had only vetoed the incense sticks.

He was standing in Andrea's kitchen, finally able to cook to his heart's content. He did not have to pay any attention to the aphrodisiac effect of the dishes, his arsenal of kitchen gadgets had grown and now his eagerness to experiment was almost limitless. He had been busy preparing this dinner for two days.

The menu consisted of his experimental versions of classic Indian dishes:

Cinnamon curry caviar chapattis

Baby snapper marinated in turmeric with molee curry sabayon

Frozen mango curry foam
Milk-fed lamb cutlets in jardaloo essence with dried apricot purée
Beech-smoked tandoori poussin on tomato, butter and pepper jelly
Kulfi with mango air

This may have been slightly shorter than the classic Love Food menu, but it was more work because each course had to be given the finishing touches just before serving. Six times over for twelve people.

Maravan was as nervous as a sprinter before the start of a race. And the fact that Andrea kept on coming in every few minutes did not make it any easier.

The milk-fed lamb cutlets were cooking in the digital water bath (one of Love Food's new acquisitions) at exactly 65 degrees, along with the tandoori poussins, another of Maravan's new creations. He was working on the curry sauce that would form the basis for the molee sabayon; the onions, which he was lightly sautéing in his *tawa* in coconut oil with chillies, garlic and ginger, had just turned a honey-yellow when Andrea came in.

'I'm amazed you don't freeze with that window open.'

He did not reply. He had told her often enough that he could not work in a jumble of smells. He always had to air his kitchen in order to separate the aromas and work with precision. He did not cook his curries by measuring amounts; he cooked them by using his nose.

And this nose was now telling him that it was exactly the time to add tomatoes, peppercorns, cloves, cardamom and curry leaves.

'When you've got a moment I'd be grateful if you could come into the sitting room.'

He must have looked irritated because she said, 'Please, I'll be quick, really quick.'

She waited for him to follow her.

They had carried the suite which made the room into a dining-cum-sitting room into the office; otherwise there would have been no room for the table for twelve. Together with the chairs, they had borrowed this from a former employer who ran a trendy pub with a garden on the edge of town. Now it was covered with a variety of Indian tablecloths which she had bought in the end from the department store that had the Indian Week. Along the entire length was a centrepiece of two white tablecloths folded lengthways. On top of this was a garland of orchids, of the sort that could be bought cheaply in Thai shops, interrupted by candles. They had stuck with the idea of candlelight.

'Well?' Andrea asked.

'Lovely,' he replied.

'Not kitschy?'

'Kitschy?' Maravan did not know this word. 'Very lovely,' he said again, and went back into the kitchen.

He retained the mini chapattis as the *amuse-bouche*. But instead of drizzling the curry leaf, cinnamon and coconut oil essence with a pipette, he took off the fat and poured the essence into calcium chloride water until it formed caviar pearls. These were then rubbed in coconut oil and used to decorate the warm mini chapattis.

He had to leave making the fake caviar to the last minute, so that the tiny balls did not set. They should be liquid inside and burst between tongue and palate. Andrea came back in again. She had her telephone in her hand and a smile of incredulity on her face. 'You're not going to believe this.'

Maravan continued working without looking up.

'Someone's just called and said, "Are you the ones who do the sex dinners?"'

'What did you tell him?'

'That he'd got the wrong number.'

'Good.'

'"This is Love Food, isn't it?" was his reply.'

'Where did he get the number from?'

'A friend of a friend.'

'Who?'

'He said that was irrelevant. "So do you do sex dinners or not?"' Andrea said it with a deep voice and in a broad, rather common accent.

'What then?'

'I said no.'

'Could you see his number on your phone?'

'Yes.'

'So find out who it was on the internet.'

'Won't work. It's a mobile number.'

It took half an hour for all the guests to arrive. Through the kitchen door Maravan could hear the piercing shrieks of people catching up with each other and the over-excited laughter of those arriving. Now and then Andrea brought an empty bottle of champagne into the kitchen and left again with a full one.

Finally she popped her head in and said, 'Go!'

This was Maravan's cue.

Almost three hours later he was sitting on a kitchen chair, satisfied with his work and the seamless progression of the courses. Then Andrea came in, beaming and slightly tipsy, took his hand, and brought him out into the dining room.

There, twelve women sitting in the flattering candlelight turned their heads to the door.

'Ladies, let me introduce to you Maestro Maravan!' Andrea proclaimed.

The cheering and applause made Maravan so embarrassed that he became stiff and serious.

Andrea received phone calls the following day, and the day after that letters from her delighted guests. Most of them said that they would be making use of Love Food's services very soon, two of them even said very, very soon. One of them had already made a firm booking: in ten days' time, on 27 November, 7.30, four people.

The success was absolutely crucial. Including the champagne and wine, Love Food had invested more than 2,000 francs in the dinner. Neither Andrea nor Maravan had any cash put by. In view of how well the business had been going they had both spent a fair amount of money. And Love Food had invested in a number of high-tech kitchen appliances, which the company would not have been able to afford in its current circumstances.

They were also forced to change their pricing. Charges for non-therapy dinners had to be lower, naturally. Andrea had calculated that they would make up for these losses with the higher numbers of guests. She had reckoned on an average of six per dinner. So the first booking for four was not a great start.

A week after the promotional dinner there had still been no further bookings. Andrea started getting nervous. She called a friend who had promised to make a reservation 'very, very soon' and said, 'I've been keeping a few evenings free for you in the next ten days and just wanted to make sure you didn't have one in mind before I give them to other people.'

'Oh,' the voice at the other end said, '*so* good of you to call. We've got a few diary difficulties at the moment. I don't want you to have to turn down other people because of me. Tell you what. Let the other people have those evenings, and as soon as we've sorted out our social calendar I'll get back to you. And if you don't have any free slots, which wouldn't surprise me, then it's my own fault.'

The other potential clients, who had said they would book 'very soon' made similar excuses when Andrea called.

25

Maravan was kneeling before his domestic shrine. His forehead touched the floor. He was praying to Lakshmi for Ulagu.

Today he had received the news that Ulagu had disappeared. In the morning he had been with his brothers and sisters; in the evening he was nowhere to be seen.

Whenever a fourteen-year-old boy disappeared in the north of Sri Lanka, the first worry was that he had died, the second that he had become a soldier, voluntarily or involuntarily joining the Tamil Tigers or the Karuna rebels fighting with the Sri Lankan army.

Maravan prayed this was not the case – that at this very moment, while he was praying for Ulagu, the boy was already back safe and sound with his family.

He could hear the ringtone of his mobile in the kitchen. He ignored it, finished his prayer, and started to sing his mantra in a restrained voice.

Afterwards, he straightened up, folded his hands across his chest, bowed and touched his forehead. He stood and went into the kitchen, back to preparing the dinner in two days' time that he had interrupted to pray.

Four iron pots were sitting on the cold stove, each with a different-coloured curry: a lamb curry with yoghurt, light brown;

a fish curry with coconut milk, yellow; a vegetable curry, green; and a Goan lobster curry, orange.

He wanted to make four jellies from these and pair each one with its main ingredient: a slice of lamb fillet cooked pink on the light brown one; a steamed halibut cheek on the yellow one; okra stuffed with lentils for the green one; and a lobster rosette for the orange one.

He relit the flames under the pans and waited, absent-mindedly, until the bubbles started rising again.

He noticed the mobile phone on the work unit. *One missed call*, it said, and a text message.

Stop. Dinner cancelled. A

Maravan went to the stove and turned off the gas. He did not care.

There was still no trace of Ulagu three days after his disappearance.

On the fourth day the Tigers arrived.

Maravan was experimenting in his kitchen with different jellification dosages when the bell rang. Two of his compatriots were standing at the door. He knew one of them: Thevaram, the LTTE man who had arranged Maravan's *modhakam* job at the temple and pocketed 1,000 francs for the favour.

The other man was holding a briefcase. Thevaram introduced him as Rathinam.

'May we come in?'

Maravan reluctantly let them in.

Thevaram glanced into the kitchen.

'Well equipped. Business seems to be doing all right.'

'What can I do for you?' Maravan asked.

'They say you've set up a catering service.'

Rathinam remained silent, just staring at Maravan.

'I cook for people sometimes,' said Maravan. 'Cooking's my profession.'

'And successfully, too. You sent more than 6,000 francs back home in the last few weeks. Congratulations!'

It came as no surprise to Maravan that the Batticaloa Bazaar had passed the details on to these people.

'My grandmother is very ill,' was all he said in reply.

'And you paid back all your loan to Ori. Congratulations again!'

Ori, too, thought Maravan. He waited.

'Yesterday was Maaveerar,' Thevaram continued, 'Heroes' Day.'

Maravan nodded.

'We wanted to bring you Velupillai Pirapaharan's speech.'

Thevaram looked at his companion. The latter opened his briefcase and took out a computer printout. At the top of the page was a portrait of the stocky LTTE leader in camouflage gear, and a long text underneath.

Maravan took the sheet of paper. The two men offered him their hands.

'Congratulations again on your success. We'll keep our fingers crossed that the authorities don't hear of your lucrative activities. Especially as you're still signing on.'

At the door Rathinam spoke for the first time: 'Read the speech. Particularly the end.' Maravan could hear their footsteps in the stairwell and then the muffled ding-dong of a doorbell one floor below.

The end of the speech went like this:

> At this historic juncture, I would request Tamils, in whatever part of the world that they may live, to raise their voices, firmly and with determination, in support of the freedom struggle of their brothers and sisters in Tamil Eelam. I would request them from my heart to strengthen the hands of our freedom movement and continue to extend their contributions and help. I would also take this opportunity to express my affection and my praise to our Tamil youth living outside our homeland for the prominent and committed role they play in actively contributing towards the liberation of our nation.
>
> Let us all make a firm and determined resolution to follow fully the path of our heroes, who, in pursuit of our aspiration for justice and freedom, sacrificed themselves and have become a part of the history of our land and our people.

Maravan went into the kitchen, threw the paper in the bin, and washed his face and hands very thoroughly. Before he entered the sitting room he took off his shoes, then he kneeled in front of the domestic shrine, lit the wick of the *deepam*, and prayed fervently that Ulagu would not follow the path of the heroes.

26

Andrea was freezing as she sat in the rattan chair in her conservatory. She wore thick woollen socks and had pulled up her legs, so the Kashmir shawl covered her toes. The shawl had been a present from Liliane, Dagmar's predecessor. Andrea had met her in Sulawesi, a happening restaurant which, with its international fusion cooking, had enjoyed a brief heyday and then vanished. Liliane, an analyst at a large bank, was a regular at Sulawesi. Andrea had served her table on her first night working there and flirted a little. When she left the restaurant long after midnight Liliane was waiting for her in her red Porsche Boxster and asked whether she could give her a lift home.

'Whose home?' Andrea had asked.

That was a long time ago now, and the Kashmir shawl had a few moth holes, which annoyed Andrea every time she took it out of the cupboard.

The November Föhn wind was shaking the rickety windows, the draught stirring the indoor palms. She had put an electric heater in the middle of the room, because the only radiator was lukewarm. It needed bleeding, but Andrea did not know how. Dagmar had always done that.

The electric heater would send her bills sky-high, but she did not care. She refused to accept that the conservatory – otherwise known as a winter garden – could not be used in winter.

She put the newspaper she had finished reading to one side and did something she had not done for weeks: she picked up the job section, which she usually threw away unread, along with the rest of the classified pages.

Love Food had a total of three bookings till the end of the year. Two on the back of her promotional dinner, and one from a couple of Esther's patients who had contacted her directly. And this was December, the high season for the catering industry.

Even if there were another one or two bookings, these would not be enough to keep Love Food afloat. Andrea saw two choices: go on the dole like Maravan or look through the job announcements. Maybe she would find something that would give her the evenings free, so she would be available for Love Food if they got a booking. She had not abandoned all hope that Esther Dubois might call again, or someone else from her clique. She still clung to the idea – her idea – of aphrodisiac catering and hoped that Maravan's residency status would soon allow them to run Love Food as an official concern.

To her mind it would have been unfair on him to give up so quickly. She felt responsible for his situation. If it were not for her he would probably still be working at the Huwyler. And, after all, it had been her fault that they no longer had bookings through Esther Dubois.

She dropped the job advertisements, pulled the shawl up to her chin and started thinking again about how to get Love Food back on its feet.

But it was a surprising call from Maravan that provided the answer.

The previous day Maravan had been standing at a snack bar at the main railway station. He was wearing a woolly hat and scarf, sipping his tea. Before him was a folded Sunday newspaper, unread, in which he had put an envelope with 3,000 francs in large denomination notes. It was practically all he had left from his Love Food income.

He had found out the day before that his sister had received a letter from Ulagu. The boy wrote that he was committed to the struggle for freedom and justice and had joined the LTTE fighters. It was his handwriting, Maravan's sister had said, but not his language.

He saw Thevaram coming. He was making his way through the passengers, idlers and those just waiting. At his side was the silent Rathinam.

They waved at him and came over to his table. Neither of them showed any inclination to get a drink from the snack bar.

Maravan pointed to the paper. Thevaram dragged it over, lifted it slightly, felt the envelope with his hand, and counted the notes without looking. Then he raised his eyebrows approvingly and said, 'Your brothers and sisters back home will thank you for this.'

Maravan sipped his tea. 'Maybe they can do something for me, too.'

'They are fighting for you,' Thevaram replied.

'I've got a nephew. He joined the fighters. He's not even fifteen.'

'There are many brave young men among our brothers.'

'He's not a young man. He's a boy.'

Thevaram and Rathinam exchanged glances.

'I will give greater support to the struggle.'

The two men exchanged glances again.

'What's his name?' Rathinam suddenly asked.

Maravan told him the name, Rathinam jotted it down in a notebook.

'Thank you,' Maravan said.

'All I've done so far is made a note of his name,' Rathinam replied.

As a result of this meeting Maravan decided to ring Andrea.

He was not sure whether Thevaram and Rathinam had any influence over Ulagu's fate, but he knew the LTTE's arm was a long one. He had heard of Tigers demanding contributions from asylum seekers, using scarcely veiled threats against relatives back home. If they were capable of threatening people's lives over such a distance, then maybe it was in their power to save them too.

Maravan had no option. He had to seize the chance, however small, that the two men could do something for Ulagu. And that cost money. More than he was earning at the moment.

The cold room smelt of heating oil. It had taken Maravan a long time to light the burner. Now, barefoot and in a sarong, he was kneeling before the domestic altar doing his *puja*. Despite the cold he was taking longer over it than usual. He prayed for Ulagu and for himself, that he might make the right decision.

When he stood up he realized the burner had gone out and the bottom of the combustion chamber was swimming in oil. He set about soaking up the oil with kitchen paper – a job he detested. When he had finally done it and the burner was lit again, Maravan and the whole flat stank of oil. He opened the windows, took a long shower, made himself some tea, then shut the windows.

Maravan pulled the chair away from the computer and over to the burner. In his leather jacket, pressing the cup of tea tightly against his torso, he sat in the weak light of the *deepam*, which was still flickering by the shrine, and thought.

Undoubtedly it was against his culture, his religion, his upbringing and his convictions. But he was not in Sri Lanka. He was in exile. You could not live here as you did at home.

How many women of the diaspora went to work, even though it was their job to run the household, bring up the children and cultivate and pass on the traditions and religious customs? But here they had to earn money. Life here forced them to.

How many asylum seekers were obliged to take jobs that were only fit for the lower castes – kitchen helps, cleaners, carers? Most of them, because life here forced them to.

How many Hindus within the diaspora had to make Sunday the holy day of their week, even though it ought to be Friday? All of them, because life here forced them to.

So why should he, Maravan, not also do something that back home would go against his culture, tradition and decency, if life in exile forced him to?

He went to the telephone and dialled Andrea's number.

'How are things looking?' was the first thing Maravan asked when Andrea answered.

She hesitated a moment before replying. 'Pretty dire, to be honest. Still only three bookings.'

It was silent on the other end for a while.

Then Maravan said, 'I think I would do it now.'

'What?'

'The dirty stuff.'

Andrea understood immediately what he was saying, but asked, 'What dirty stuff?'

Maravan paused.

'If someone else rings and wants, you know, sex dinners. As far as I'm concerned you can say yes.'

'Oh that. All right, I'll take that on board. Anything else?'

'Nothing.'

As soon as Maravan had hung up, she looked for the number of the caller who had asked about the sex dinners. She had noted it down, just in case.

December 2008

27

The apartment in Falkengässchen was on the fourth floor, right in the middle of the old town in a lavishly restored seventeenth-century house, if the inscription above the door was to be believed. A new, silent lift had brought her up here. The sitting room and kitchen took up the entire floor. The sloping roof went right up into the gable and opened out onto a roof terrace, from where you could look out over the tiled roofs and church towers of the old town.

A door in the wall led to the adjacent building. Behind it were two large bedrooms, each with a suite of furniture, and a luxurious bathroom. Everything was new and expensive, but kitted out in bad taste. Plenty of marble and gold-plated fittings, deep-pile carpets, dubious antiques and chrome-steel furniture, bowls with dried, perfumed petals.

The apartment reminded Andrea of a hotel suite. It did not look as if anybody lived there.

When she rang the man who had asked about 'sex dinners' that time, he answered with a brusque 'Yes?' His name was Rohrer and he came to the point immediately. They – he did not reveal who 'they' were – occasionally organized private dinners for relaxation. The guests were people for whom discretion was crucial. If she thought she might be able to offer something in this line, he would arrange a test dinner. Depending on the result, this might lead to further dinners.

Andrea met Rohrer the very next day to look around the premises. A man in his late thirties with short-cropped hair, he scrutinized her with a professional gaze. She was a head taller than him, and in the cramped lift up to the apartment she could smell a mixture of sweat and Paco Rabanne.

She told him that the apartment was suitable and that the suggested date in four days' time – she looked awkwardly in her diary – was possible.

The dinner was served in the bedroom. The suite had been removed and Andrea had made the usual table with cloths and cushions – including brass fingerbowls, as now diners would be eating with their hands again.

For the first time Maravan worked with a tall chef's hat. Andrea had insisted on it, and at the moment he did not feel like putting up a fight.

The dinner was planned for a woman and a man. Rohrer would leave the moment the guests arrived. But Andrea and Maravan should stay after the last course, until they were called.

He cooked his standard menu. With the usual care, but without the usual passion, Andrea thought.

*

The man was Rohrer's boss. He was in his early fifties, somewhat overly groomed, wearing a blazer with golden buttons, grey gabardine trousers and a blue-and-white striped shirt, the white high collar of which was fastened by a gold pin. It made a bridge below the knot of his yellow tie.

He had green eyes and reddish, slightly longish hair, styled back with gel. Andrea noticed his fingernails. They were carefully manicured and polished.

He glanced into the kitchen, said hello to Andrea and Maravan, and introduced himself as Kull. René Kull.

They did not see his companion until they brought out the champagne. She was sitting at the dressing table, her narrow back in a low-cut dress facing Andrea. Her hair was shaven to within millimetres and went down in a wedge shape to the bottom of her neck. Her skin was a deep ebony colour, which shone in the light of Andrea's sea of candles.

When she turned round, Andrea saw a roundish forehead of the sort that women from Ethiopia or Sudan have. Her full lips were painted red and now puckered into a surprised, interested smile.

Andrea beamed back. She had not seen such a beautiful woman for a long time. Her name was Makeda. Makeda set about the dinner with such pleasure and gusto that Andrea wondered whether she might not be a prostitute. Kull, on the other hand, kept his composure, not even unbuttoning that collar which had already seemed as if it might choke him when he arrived.

When they had not heard the temple bell for a while after the confectionery, Andrea listened anxiously to the noises coming out of the room. Then Kull strode into the kitchen.

'Of course, the main reason for the effect this dinner has is the knowledge that you're eating an erotic menu – and all the other stuff, the candles, eating with your hands. But do you actually put something else in the food?' Kull's cheeks were slightly red, but his top button was still done up.

'I don't put anything else in the food,' Maravan explained. 'It's what's in there already that creates the effect.'

'And what's that?'

'Herr Kull,' Andrea interjected, 'I'm sure you'll understand that that's our professional secret.'

Kull nodded. 'Are you just as discreet in other ways?' he asked after a while.

28

From that point onwards Love Food cooked regularly for Kull. The venue was always the apartment in Falkengässchen. Only the guests changed. Especially the men.

René Kull ran an escort service for a very upmarket, mostly international clientele. Men whose business brought them to the financial centre or the headquarters of the International Football Federation, or those who were simply making a stop on their way to a family holiday in the mountains. They set great store by discretion and were not infrequently accompanied by hefty, taciturn men who would munch on sandwiches they had brought with them in the sitting room.

Kull did not quibble about the price Andrea had tentatively asked for: 2,000 plus drinks.

Andrea had never come into contact with this world before, and she was fascinated. She was quick to strike up conversation with the women, who usually arrived before their clients and would have a drink and a few cigarettes in the sitting room while waiting. They were beautiful, wore off-the-peg clothes and expensive jewellery, and treated her as if she were one of their own. She enjoyed chatting to them. They were funny and talked about their work with an ironic distance which made Andrea laugh.

The women loved these evenings because of the food. And because – as a Brazilian girl confessed – it even made what came afterwards quite fun.

Andrea had little to do with the men. They usually turned up accompanied by Rohrer, Kull's dogsbody, who would bring them straight into the prepared room, then disappear immediately. When Andrea served up the dishes, she would focus her attention on their female companions.

On one occasion she was banished to the kitchen with Maravan. There was a huge commotion in Falkengässchen before the guest arrived. A number of bodyguards searched the apartment, one making a recce of the kitchen, and after the mystery person had been smuggled past the closed kitchen door, yet another bodyguard came in and announced that he would be doing the waiting. All Andrea had to do was explain to him what each dish was. Each time he had served one, he practised the presentation of the following one with her until the temple bell rang again.

'I'd love to know who that was,' Andrea said as she and Maravan were going down in the lift.

'I wouldn't,' Maravan replied.

It was not the shady side of his work that bothered Maravan, it was his role in it. When the diners had been for couples in therapy, he had been treated with the respect afforded to a doctor or specialist who is in a position to help people. And when they had done normal catering assignments he had been feted like a star.

Here he was ignored totally. It didn't matter how tall his chef's hat was, he was invisible. He hardly ever came face to face with the guests, and Andrea never had any compliments to relay back to him when she brought in the dirty crockery.

As a kitchen help Maravan had been used to leading a shadowy existence. But this was different: the guests came here because of his creations. Whatever happened between them was a direct result of his artistry. In short, the artist in Maravan felt neglected. And, what was almost worse, so did the man.

His relationship with Andrea had not developed in the way he wanted. He hoped that being together almost every day, the close contact and the conspiratorial nature of their collaboration, would bring them closer. It did, but only as friends, almost like siblings. The erotic element of their work did not rub off on their relationship.

However, whereas Andrea felt nothing more than friendship towards Maravan, she became very close with the girls working for Kull. By the second meeting they were already hugging each other like long-lost friends, spending the time before the punters – Maravan deliberately called them this in front of Andrea – arrived chatting, smoking and laughing on the white sofas. There was one girl in particular she liked: a tall Ethiopian called Makeda. If Maravan was honest, he felt jealous of this woman.

Makeda had fled to Britain with her mother and older sister when she was twelve. They belonged to the Oromo people; her father had joined its liberation movement, the Oromo Liberation Front.

After the fall of the Derg government he was an OLF deputy in the transition parliament, but following the elections the OLF left the Government and put itself in opposition to the ruling party.

Early one morning soldiers had arrived at Makeda's parents' house, ransacked the place and taken away her father. It was the last time she saw him. Her mother made dogged attempts to discover where he was being held, and thanks to some former acquaintances she did indeed find out. Her contacts even allowed her to visit the prison. She returned home silent and red-eyed. Two days later, Makeda, her mother and sister crossed the Kenyan border in a clapped-out Land Rover. From that point on, her mother could not call in any more favours from old acquaintances. They flew to London and sought asylum. They never heard from her father again.

At sixteen Makeda was discovered by a modelling agency scout. He called her 'the new Naomi Campbell'. Against her mother's will, she went to a few castings, took part in some fashion shows and was photographed for magazines. But she waited in vain for the breakthrough.

It was during Milan Fashion Week that she crossed the fine line between up-and-coming model and call girl. Feeling lonely, she took a purchaser for a boutique chain back to her room. When she awoke the following morning he was gone. On the bedside table were 500 euros. 'I then realized that my first lover had also been my first punter,' she said with a sarcastic laugh.

When she had to accept that she was not going to get very far as a model, Makeda went back to her family and to school. But by now she was used to a freer and more expensive existence. Life was too constricted at home; she found her mother's views too narrow-minded. It was not long before they were arguing. Makeda moved out, for good.

She was discovered by another scout, but this time they worked for an escort service. Makeda became a call girl, a profession in which she met with rather more success than on the catwalk.

Makeda had come across Kull less than a year ago. He lured her away and she followed him to Switzerland, where she felt pretty lonely.

She related all of this in the half-light of Andrea's bedroom. While waiting for a client they had made a date for the following day. Despite the cold, they went for a walk by the lake and ended up in Andrea's bed, as if this were the natural order of things.

So Maravan's jealousy was not unjustified. Andrea was in love.

Not long after their last visit, Thevaram and Rathinam were back at Maravan's flat. They brought news from Ulagu. They claimed he had signed up for the Black Tigers, an elite unit of suicide bombers. The entry requirements were very tough, however; there was a good chance he would be rejected. They could try to increase this chance through their contacts, if Maravan so wished.

Maravan promised them another donation of 2,000 francs.

After their visit, Maravan let his sister know, via the Batticaloa Bazaar, that he had made some initial progress in the matter they had discussed.

*

The Huwyler was normally booked out in December; both rooms would be full almost every night. But this year a few of the stalwart companies who always took the restaurant for their Christmas management dinners had not made reservations. Huwyler was convinced they were either using the crisis as an excuse or had come to this decision for appearance's sake: it did not look very good if you started tightening your belt, but dined at the Huwyler.

Whichever it was, it amounted to the same thing for Huwyler. The restaurant had noticeably fewer customers than usual at this time of year.

This is why he was paying particular attention to Staffel's table. It had twelve diners: top management and their wives, a real rarity these days.

Staffel had every reason to celebrate. The financial press had unanimously voted him Manager of the Year in the 'new technology' division. And the company he ran, Kugag, had registered such good results that both they and their image could afford themselves this little luxury.

He could have been a little more generous in his choice of menu, however. Huwyler had suggested the tasting menu, but Staffel had opted for a simple six-courser. He stuck to the mid-price wines, too. In these times it was the prudent, conventional types who became Managers of the Year.

By contrast, another of his guests was anything but prudent or conventional: Dalmann, the heart-attack victim. The first time he showed his face in the restaurant, fresh from his rehabilitation, less than a month after the attack, Huwyler was shocked. Less by his audacity at turning up here at all after that distressing incident, but by the fact that Dalmann could actually do it all over again. He did not hold back with the food or drink, and even ordered a cigar to go with his cognac.

Since then, however, Dalmann had become a very welcome guest. A sign of normality.

He was here this evening, too. In the company of Dr Neller, business lawyer and – as the two men kept emphasizing with ever greater frequency as the evening wore on – a childhood friend and a fellow Boy Scout. They ate the *Surprise*.

Dalmann pulled a fir twig from the Christmas table decoration with the dark-blue bauble and held it above the candle. He loved the fragrance of singed pine needles. The essence of Christmas. It made him feel sentimental in a nice way, especially on an evening like this, after a good dinner with an old friend. The restaurant was not too full or too empty, not too loud or too quiet. The smoke of his Bahia was cool, the Armagnac smooth and the conversation friendly.

'Have you made use of Kull's services again?' Neller enquired.

Dalmann smiled. 'I've got to watch my heart, you know that.'

'Of course. I always forget that when I see you like this.'

'Why do you ask? Should I be?'

'I don't want to put your life at risk, but in case you do fancy it, he's offering something with food now.'

'I'd rather eat here.'

'It's a very special dinner. Erotic.'

Dalmann gave him a quizzical look and puffed on his cigar.

'He's got an Indian or someone like that who cooks and a hot bird who serves it up. By the way, she used to wait here briefly, you know: tall, black hair all combed to one side.'

'And now she's working for Kull?'

'Only as a waitress.'

'And she's responsible for the erotic bit?'

'No, it's the food that does that. I didn't believe it to begin with either. But it's true. The food makes you feel completely different.'

'In what way?'

'Not just excited down there,' Neller pointed vaguely downwards. 'That, too. But more up here.' He tapped his high forehead, which was glistening with sweat.

'You mean you get a stiffy in your head?' Dalmann laughed, but Neller seemed to think about his question quite seriously.

'Yes, you could put it like that. And the best thing about it is that it appears to turn the women on too. You get the impression they're actually enjoying it.'

'They're paid to act like they are.'

Neller shook his head. 'Take the word of an old fox. I can tell the difference. It's real. Maybe not completely, but definitely a little bit.'

Dalmann chewed thoughtfully. Then he wiped his mouth and asked, 'Do you think they put something in the food?'

'They say they don't. It's just the recipes. And the ambience. Cushions and candles. You sit on the floor and eat with your hands.'

'What do you eat?'

'Spicy stuff. Spicy and sweet. It's a sort of Ayurvedic molecular cuisine. Strange, but outstanding. Special tip from me. Not cheap, mind, but something totally different.'

'And definitely no drugs or chemicals?'

'All I can say is that I felt brilliant the following morning. And – just between us chaps – I haven't had a shag like that in a long time.'

'As I said, my heart.'

Neller raised both hands. 'I'm just telling you, Eric. Just telling you.'

Dalmann had no intention of following up his friend's tip. But he would happily bear it in mind if he ever needed anything really special for someone.

They changed the subject and went on chatting for a while. When Huwyler accompanied them to a taxi with an umbrella, snow had settled on the entryway. And large, heavy flakes of snow were still falling.

On the evening when they had been celebrating their year-end results and the Manager of the Year award, Dalmann had come to the table, congratulated Staffel and said, 'Thanks to you I've won a large bet.'

'A bet?' Staffel asked.

'I bet that it would be you.'

'Well, that was quite a gamble. I hope the wager wasn't too high.'

'Six bottles of Cheval Blanc '97. But there was no risk. I hope you have a good dinner, ladies and gentlemen. Enjoy your evening, you've deserved it.'

'Isn't that the chap who came over last time and knew more than I did?' Staffel's wife had whispered to her husband the moment Dalmann left their table. 'Do you know who he is now?'

Staffel had enquired, but could not say much about him. Dalmann was a lawyer, but did not practise as one. He sat on a number of boards and worked as a consultant and intermediary. He forged business relationships, brought people together, stepped in sometimes, too, if a post had to be refilled informally, and obviously had such good contacts in the media that he could get certain snippets of inside information if necessary.

Staffel ought to get to know Dalmann better.

29

As the year came to a close, it was difficult to say which was greater: relief that it was over or worry about what the next year would bring.

The state of the global markets was cataclysmic: the Swiss stock exchange had experienced its worst year since 1974; the DAX had collapsed by 40 per cent; the Dow Jones had lost more than a third of its value; the Nikkei registered similar losses; the stock exchange in Shanghai had plummeted by 65 per cent; and Russia had put all these in the shade with a fall in stocks of 72 per cent.

It was the last of these that had a particularly visible impact on Kull's sector. The Russians had been good clients in the last few years. Usually, over the holiday period, a large proportion of his team's work would be shifted to St Moritz and he would have to call in extra staff to meet the demand. But this year the advance bookings suggested there would be little need for that.

By contrast, the Love Food business had been going so well that Kull wanted to make it available in the Engadin Valley as well. To be on the safe side he had already booked the duo for a few days.

For Dalmann, the holiday period in St Moritz was the most important business event of the year. It provided an opportunity to meet people with whom it was impossible to have personal contact throughout the rest of the year. He could revive old connections and secure new ones. A multitude of social occasions made it possible to come together in an informal, relaxed atmosphere, get closer to people personally, and pave the way for new deals or maintain old ones.

Up in the mountains the crisis had made itself felt, too, but it was as Dalmann had expected: the quality guests still came this year. The crisis had the advantage of separating the wheat from the chaff.

He stayed as usual in the Chesa Clara, in a five-room apartment on the top floor. A dentist friend had built the house at the beginning of the 1990s; since then Dalmann had rented every year during the Christmas holidays. It was a considerable expense, but one which had always paid off in the past. He hoped it would this time, too.

The apartment was slightly over-furnished and fitted with old walnut doors and pine panelling, which had been collected from a variety of ancient houses. It was roomy enough for Dalmann and two guests, and also had a small staff flat where Lourdes stayed. She did the housework and also made breakfast here. She did not have to cook, because he always ate out and never invited people over to dinner. Apart from his legendary hangover breakfast on New Year's Day: open house from eleven o'clock until dusk.

He rarely engaged in any sporting activities these days. In the past he had been an excellent skier, but now he would only put on skis to make it up to those mountain restaurants that were not accessible on foot. Otherwise he preferred to take gentle walks to culinary destinations. Or go to the same establishments by horse-drawn sleigh.

It was Maravan's first time in the mountains. Throughout the entire journey he was silent and sceptical, sitting in the passenger seat of Andrea's packed estate car. When the hills around them became taller and more rugged, the roads narrower and lined with snow, when it actually started snowing, he regretted agreeing to go on this adventure.

When they reached their destination, he was disappointed to see just another town, no more beautiful than the one they had left, but smaller, colder, wedged between mountains and with more snow.

Where they were staying was not much nicer than Theodorstrasse, either. Each of them had a tiny studio in a block of flats with a view of another block.

Shortly after their arrival, however, Andrea knocked on Maravan's door and persuaded him to come on an excursion. They drove further along the valley, southwards.

They stopped in a village called Maloja. 'If we continued on this road for about an hour you'd see palm trees.'

'Let's go on then,' he suggested, half-seriously.

Andrea laughed and walked in front.

The path soon became narrow, bounded by walls of snow. Maravan found it difficult to keep up. He was wearing clunky rubber and nylon boots without any grip. He had bought them in the same cheap department store that he bought everything, save for those items he needed for his kitchen. His trousers were so tight they would not go over the tops of his boots; he had to stuff them inside, which must have looked ridiculous. He could not be absolutely sure, however, because where he was staying there was no mirror in which he could see his feet.

The firs that lined the path were heavily laden with snow. Now and then some fell to the ground. This was followed by a trickle of white glitter from the branches relieved of their burden.

All he could hear was the crunching of their shoes. When Andrea stopped and waited for him, he stopped too. That was the first time he heard silence.

It was a silence that engulfed everything. A silence that became more powerful every second.

He had never been so aware just how remorselessly his entire life had been full of noise. The chitter-chatter of his family, the hooting of the traffic, the wind in the palms, the crashing of waves in the Indian Ocean, the explosions of the civil war, the clattering in kitchens, the sing-song of the temple, the rattle of the trams, the droning of traffic, the chitter-chatter of his thoughts.

Now, all of a sudden, there was silence. Like a jewel. Like a luxury item people like him had no right to.

'What's wrong?' Andrea asked. 'Are you coming?'

'Shh!' he said, putting his forefinger to his lips.

But the silence had vanished, like a timid animal.

Andrea reproached herself for having dragged Maravan up here. She could see how uncomfortable he felt. In the snow he was like a cat in the rain.

He was out of place in this landscape. When she thought about how gracefully he moved in his sarong, how elegantly in his long apron, wearing the white forage cap. Here, in his shapeless windcheater, his woolly hat pulled down over his ears, and wearing cheap snow boots, he was as stripped of his dignity as a zoo animal of its freedom.

What pained her most was that he knew all this. He bore it with the same resignation with which he had borne everything since he had decided to get involved with the dirty stuff, as he called it.

She did not fool herself about his feelings for her either. The longer they worked together the more obvious it became that he was in love with her. He had taken what she privately called 'the incident' more seriously than she had imagined. She sensed that he had not given up hope that he might win her round again, maybe even for good.

As soon as she was sure what his feelings were, she had started to distance herself from him. She had deliberately refrained from being too friendly, in case he misunderstood her. Her behaviour towards him was cordial but non-committal, and although she sensed this hurt him, the clarity it created was good for their work.

Since Makeda, the relationship had become complicated again, however. Maravan was showing all the symptoms of jealousy. Although she felt sorry for him, she did not see how she could possibly help.

Quite the opposite, in fact. Andrea was feeling particularly pleased about things, because Makeda was here too. She was staying with the other girls who worked for Kull in a nearby apartment building. They had planned to spend as much time together as they could.

Maravan was aware of this. To cheer him up, Andrea had taken him on this trip as soon as they had unpacked their things.

Maravan had dropped back and for a while stood motionless in this fairytale landscape. She had called him, but he had told her gruffly to be quiet. He lingered there as if listening to something. Andrea listened, too, but could hear nothing.

Finally he got going again and made his way towards her. When he arrived he smiled.

'Beautiful,' he said.

30

Two of Dalmann's strengths – luck and a memory for faces – worked in combination to ensure that his stay at Chesa Clara had paid for itself within a few days.

There had not been a winter like this for ages: cold, white and blue, and a volume of snow that nobody had seen up here at this time of year.

Dalmann was sitting on the sun terrace of a mountain restaurant deep down in a valley. He was there with Rolf Schär, the same dentist friend who owned the apartment. It was not a particularly efficient pairing as far as business was concerned, but not totally useless either, because Dalmann knew that Schär could get a much higher rent for the location during this high-season period. This is why he had forced himself to spend some time with him at least once during his stay.

The two men were feeling relaxed as they sat on their bench by the wooden façade of the building, their faces glistening with sun cream in the winter sun, drinking a bottle of Grüner Veltliner and picking at the plate of cold meats on the table in front of them. From time to time one of them would say something, usually what was on their mind at that moment, like elderly people who have known each other for years and have no need for any pretence.

As they watched children sledging beyond the terrace, Schär said, 'The snow seems much higher when you're small.' Dalmann's attention was distracted by a group of people just arriving. Four men around fifty who looked as though they might be Arabs. They were shown to the neighbouring table, which had been expecting its guests for a while – it was the only one with a reserved sign.

Briefly removing his sunglasses and glancing at the other guests, Dalmann recognized one of them: the right-hand man of Jafar Fajahat, another individual for whom Palucron had once helped broker deals. He was around ten years older than when he had last seen him, but it was definitely the same man.

After Musharaff's resignation Dalmann had no longer been able to contact Fajahat, and he supposed he had fallen victim to the regime change. But his assistant must have survived; how otherwise could he afford to be here?

If only he could remember his name. Khalid, Khalil, Khalig or something like that. Dalmann resisted the urge to talk to him. Who on earth were the other three?

He tried to catch his gaze, and succeeded after a short while. The man took off his glasses, gave him an enquiring look, and when Dalmann nodded and smiled he stood up and greeted him in English. 'Herr Dalmann? How nice to see you. Kazi Razzaq, do you remember?'

'Of course I do.' For the time being Dalmann avoided mentioning Jafar Fajahat.

Razzaq introduced his three companions, whose names Dalmann made no effort to remember, and he introduced

Schär. A short silence ensued, as is usual after these sorts of introductions.

Dalmann broke it. 'Are you around for a few days?' he enquired.

The four men nodded.

'Good, then maybe we can do something together. Which hotel are you in?'

The four men exchanged glances.

'Tell you what, I'll give you my card. My mobile number. Call me and we'll arrange something. I'd really like to.'

Dalmann gave Razzaq his card in the hope that he would feel obliged to give him one in return. But he just thanked Dalmann, put the card away and turned to the waitress in traditional costume who was ready to take their order.

That same evening, however, Razzaq did call. They arranged to meet in the bar of one of the large five-star hotels with a view over the lake. Dalmann knew the barman and had his regular table in a quiet corner not too near the piano.

Having arrived slightly too early, he was now sipping a Campari and soda and nibbling on some warm salted almonds. It was that interval between après-ski and aperitif, Dalmann's favourite time. Most of the hotel guests were in their rooms, recovering from the day and freshening up for the evening. The pianist was playing soft, sentimental tunes; the waiters had time for a quick chat.

Razzaq arrived punctually and ordered a cola. He was one of those Muslims who did not drink, even when abroad.

Now they were alone, Dalmann enquired about Jafar Fajahat.

'He's not working any more. He's enjoying the fruits of his labour and his grandchildren. He's got fifteen of them.'

They swapped some old tales and Dalmann let the conversation slowly peter out to give his guest the opportunity to come to the point. Razzaq did not beat about the bush.

'You know how you'd occasionally put us in touch with women?'

Dalmann corrected him. 'That's not my area. What I did was put you in touch with someone who, maybe, occasionally put you in touch with women.'

Razzaq ignored this remark. 'Would it be possible here too?'

Dalmann leaned back in the small armchair and acted as if he had to consider the matter. Then he said, 'I'll see what can be done. When would this be for?'

'Tomorrow, the day after. We're here for another six days.'

Dalmann made a mental note of this. He had earned himself the right to ask a question of his own. 'Do you still work in security and defence?' he wanted to know. When Razzaq answered yes, he enquired sensitively, 'Is our government's change in strategy causing you a major headache?'

'It's not only unfair and short-sighted, it's also very bad for security. And for business.'

That year Pakistan had been the largest importer of arms from Switzerland – 110 million francs' worth. But at present the Swiss Government was holding back its approval of new exports.

'Public pressure is immense at the moment. There's soon going to be a referendum on whether to ban the export of arms. When it fails – and it definitely *is* going to fail – the situation will ease.'

Then Dalmann started talking about the disused M113 armoured personnel carriers and the perfectly legal possibility of importing these via the United States. He did not neglect to mention the role he could play in such a deal.

Dalmann spent the evening at a reception held by an auction house presenting the best pieces in its forthcoming auction of works by New York expressionists. After that he had dinner – a cheese fondue in a very simple restaurant, with a small, highly international group of acquaintances. A convivial gathering with an old tradition: anybody uttering the slightest word over dinner about business had to buy a bottle of wine as punishment. It was permitted, on the other hand, to arrange subsequent meetings to discuss such matters.

Dalmann had delegated Kazi Razzaq's request to Schaeffer. Although Dalmann knew Kull, he would not in any circumstances allow himself to be seen with the man.

He had told Schaeffer to come the following morning at ten o'clock. He received him in his dressing gown while having breakfast.

Naturally, his colleague had already eaten breakfast; he asked Lourdes for a cup of tea and an apple, which he once again peeled with that unnerving meticulousness.

'Almost there,' Dalmann said. 'Just give me a moment to thin the blood, separate the platelets, regulate the heart rhythm, and lower the blood pressure, cholesterol and uric acid levels.'

While his boss, in sheer disgust, washed down his collection of medicines with orange juice, Schaeffer used the time to tilt back his head and put drops in each eye.

'Well?' Dalmann asked.

Schaeffer dabbed his eyes with a folded handkerchief. 'Absolutely possible, he says.'

'With the Pakistani menu, too?'

'That too.'

Dalmann had charged Schaeffer with finding out whether Kull could also lay on a normal Pakistani menu for five people, served at a normal table with cutlery. The women could look after the erotic side – they would join the men for dessert and then return with them to the hotel. He wanted to broker a deal, not an orgy. He was not running a brothel after all.

'Time?'

'The caterers are free the day after tomorrow. But we shall have to let them know in the morning.'

Dalmann manoeuvred the yolk of his fried egg, which he had separated from the white, onto his piece of toast. Out of consideration for his health he did not touch the fried bacon – every other day. It was seriously difficult.

'That's decided then,' he said, putting the piece of toast into his mouth.

31

And so it happened that Maravan, the Tamil, unaware of what was going on behind the scenes, ended up cooking dinner for Razzaq, the Pakistani, a dinner during which a deal was struck that, via a circuitous route, would supply the Sri Lankan army with disused Swiss armoured personnel carriers.

The client wanted to surprise his guest with a classic Pakistani menu. Maravan allowed himself to add a few surprises.

His take on *arhar* dal, a classic lentil dish, was a ring of dal risotto served with coriander air and lemon foam.

With a little gelatine he turned the *nihari*, a beef curry cooked on the lowest heat for six hours, into *nihari praliné*, and combined it with an onion emulsion and onion crisps on rice purée.

The chicken for the biryani was vacuum-packed, cooked at a low temperature and served in a spicy palm-sugar crust made with the biryani spice mixture – accompanied by peppermint air and cinnamon ice cream.

Happy to be cooking something different, Maravan worked with great concentration in the kitchen, which was poorly equipped, but jazzed up with plenty of granite and artificially aged wood.

A certain Herr Schaeffer – a gaunt, stiff man – had met them at the door and given them all the instructions he could. He would be out for the afternoon, he told them, but Frau Lourdes was on hand. The host for the dinner was due to arrive at seven; the guests at half past.

The dinner had been ordered for five people, dessert for ten. As Kull had put it, five women would be joining them for dessert. This should consist of the usual confectionery from the Love Food menu. 'Right, so the jellied asparagus and ghee penises, and the glazed chick pea, ginger and pepper pussies,' Andrea had specified as she wrote down the order. 'And the liquorice, honey and ghee ice lollies.'

Shortly after seven Andrea came into the kitchen. 'Do you know who the host is? Dalmann.'

The name meant nothing to Maravan.

'Dalmann from the Huwyler. You know, that rather lewd old bloke at table one.'

He shook his head. 'Maybe if I saw him.'

But Maravan saw as little of Dalmann that evening as he did the other guests.

The bell rang at half past nine. Maravan could hear laughter and the buzz of conversation. The women had arrived for dessert.

Andrea entered the kitchen and quickly closed the door behind her.

'Guess who.'

'Makeda?'

Andrea nodded. After that she did not say a word.

Shortly after dessert the men left with their women. Maravan and Andrea finished too. There was a single coat hanging in the cloakroom. Andrea recognized it as Makeda's.

*

Nobody had booked Love Food for New Year's Eve 2008. On the single hob in his studio's kitchenette Maravan had cooked a classic *Kozhi Kari*, a chicken curry recipe Nangay had taught him when he was still a boy, with the usual ingredients plus a few more fenugreek seeds. He also put an extra pinch of cinnamon, as his teacher had always done, in the spice mixture of ground fennel seeds, cardamom seeds and cloves, before adding lemon juice.

Andrea was a work widow, as she called it. Makeda was booked. They had parted company an hour ago. Makeda was wearing a long, black, high-necked dress and it drove Andrea mad to think she would be spending the night with one of the elderly plutocrats who seemed to be everywhere.

Andrea had contributed the drinks for the lonely hearts' New Year's Eve party: two bottles of champagne for herself and two bottles of mineral water for Maravan. Sparkling.

She sat on the only chair in the room, Maravan on the bed. The small, round coffee table stood between them.

The room was cold. To satisfy his obsession that it should not smell of food, Maravan had kept all the windows open until shortly before she arrived. It must have been minus fifteen outside. She had to ask him for his blanket, which she now wore around her shoulders like a stole.

They ate with their hands, like the first time. The curry tasted like something from her childhood. And yet they had never eaten curry when she was younger – except for a dish in a restaurant chain that went by the name of 'Riz Colonial', a ring of rice with strips of chicken in a yellow sauce with lots of cream and tinned fruit.

She told this to Maravan.

'Maybe it's the cinnamon,' he said. 'There's lots of cinnamon in there.'

Exactly, it was the cinnamon. Rice pudding with sugar and cinnamon, one of her favourite dishes as a child. And Christmas biscuits. And *Lebkuchen*. 'Is it New Year's Eve in Sri Lanka too?'

'In Colombo, before the war, we used to celebrate religious festivals of all faiths. Hindu, Buddhist, Muslim and Christian. We got the day off school for all of them. On New Year's Eve we'd be on the streets letting off fireworks.'

'Wonderful. Do you think it will ever be like that again?'

Marvan thought long and hard. 'No,' he said finally. 'Nothing is ever what it once was.'

Andrea thought about this. 'You're right,' she said. 'But sometimes it's even better.'

'I've never had that experience myself.'

'Isn't what we're doing now better than the Huwyler?'

Maravan shrugged his shoulders. 'The work is, definitely. But I've got more worries.' And he told her about Ulagu, his favourite nephew who had become a child soldier.

'And there's nothing you can do about it?' Andrea asked when he had finished.

'Yes, I am doing something. But whether it will help . . .'

'Why don't you have a wife?' Andrea asked after a while.

Maravan gave her a meaningful smile and did not say anything.

She understood. 'No, Maravan. Get it out of your head. I'm taken.'

'By a woman who sleeps with men.'

'For money.'

'Even worse.'

Andrea became angry. 'Well, you do things for money that you wouldn't normally do either.'

Maravan made a movement with his head that was halfway between a nod and a shake.

'I never know what that means with you lot. Yes or no?'

'In my culture it's impolite to say no.'

'Not exactly easy for a girl then.' She laughed. 'And yet you don't have a girlfriend.'

Maravan remained serious. 'Back home the parents arrange the marriages.'

'In the twenty-first century? You're pulling my leg.'

Maravan shrugged.

'And you let that happen?'

'It seems to work.'

Andrea shook her head in disbelief. 'So why has nobody arranged one for you yet?'

'I don't have any parents and I don't have family here. Nobody who can testify that I'm not divorced or have illegitimate children or am not leading an immoral existence, or that I'm of the right caste.'

'I thought they abolished the caste system.'

'They did. But you have to be in the right abolished caste.'

'Which abolished caste are you in?'

'You never ask someone that.'

'How do you find out then?'

'You ask someone else.'

Andrea laughed and changed the subject. 'Shall we go outside and watch the fireworks?'

Maravan shook his head. 'I'm frightened of explosions.'

It had started snowing again. The rockets glowed, swirled and sparkled behind a veil of snowflakes, some of which were tinged green, red or yellow.

The church bells rang out the new year, a year about which the only certainty was that it would last a single second longer than the previous one.

Dalmann was celebrating in one of the Palace Hotels and was now walking beside Schelbert, an investor from northern Germany, through the noisy lobby full of décolletés, miniskirts and stilettos.

'Ghastly fashion this season,' Schelbert sighed. 'How will I recognize the tarts now?'

'They're the ones who don't look like tarts.'

January 2009

32

It was not long before Andrea saw Herr Schaeffer again.

They were making their final preparations for a Love Food menu for four people in Falkengässchen. She was just about to light the candles when she realized her lighter had run out of fuel and she could not find the box of matches she usually had to hand for such an eventuality.

The kitchen had no gas stove, and there were no lighters or matches in the drawers. She looked through the furniture in the other rooms, but found nothing.

'I'm just going to pop to the bar opposite,' she said to Maravan, slipping her coat over her sari. She went down in the lift, crossed the street and got a book of matches from the barman. When she left the bar she could see the two of them coming, more than a quarter of an hour early. She ran to the door and just got there before they did. She went up, threw her coat onto a kitchen chair, and asked Maravan to let the guests in while she lit the candles.

She had recognized one of them: Schaeffer, Dalmann's dogsbody. She thought she knew the other man, too.

When the candles were alight and the man had greeted her in a thick Dutch accent, she remembered where she had seen him before: in the Huwyler. Schaeffer had shown him the way, but had not come up with him.

Having checked to see he was the first to arrive, the Dutchman was shown the room where dinner would be served, whistled his approval, and insisted on waiting for his guest in the sitting room.

The other man arrived before the women. Andrea had seen him at the Huwyler, too. He was a slightly portly chap in his late forties with a hedgehog haircut. He was wearing a dark blue business suit with trousers that were slightly too short, and he looked embarrassed.

'How exciting!' he said several times as the two of them were taken into the room. Just like Esther Dubois before the first test dinner.

It would have been easy to cancel, and now Staffel regretted not having done so. He felt the same as he had done with his first cigarette aged fifteen. His parents had said they would give him 10,000 francs by the time he was twenty if he had never smoked. He was still convinced it was this agreement that had caused his moment of weakness back then. He had got away with it; they never found out. Nor the other times. And he had wisely invested the 10,000 francs in hardware and software while studying engineering.

There was one other occasion when he had felt like this: in Denver about eight years ago. Not wanting to appear dull, he had gone with the other guys to a table-dancing club. He must have drunk far too much and had woken up in his hotel room at five o'clock the following morning next to a fake blonde whose perfume he was only able to eradicate from his suit using an express cleaning service.

He had got away with this incident as well. Béatrice had never found out.

He would make sure this evening remained under wraps, too.

Dalmann had been in touch shortly after their second meeting in the Huwyler. He said he was a friend of van Genderen, who just happened to be in the country at the moment and would like to meet him.

Of course, Staffel knew who van Genderen was. The Number Two at hoogteco, a large supplier in the renewable energies sector. There could be no harm in having an informal meeting with this major Dutch competitor.

They had agreed, therefore, to have a drink in Dalmann's beautiful house overlooking the lake. The two men hit it off and arranged to have dinner the following evening.

They had enjoyed an excellent Japanese meal, spoken hardly a word about business, and laughed a lot. Van Genderen had a more inexhaustible repertoire of jokes than anybody he had come across since Hofer, a former comrade of his at military training school.

As the evening went on the anecdotes became more risqué, and then they started talking about risqué matters in general – which is how they arranged the dinner that, in van Genderen's words, was 'spicy in every way'.

Now that he was being served champagne in a luxury apartment in the old town by a pretty Indian girl – or was she not Indian? –

talking Swiss German, Staffel was already feeling slightly queasy. And jittery too.

He would go along with it until it got too colourful and then stop. That way nothing could happen.

This time it was no surprise that Makeda was one of the party. She had told Andrea beforehand.

Just before the new year they had their first argument. Andrea had said, 'Please stop it. I'm earning enough for two.'

'Am I hearing you right?' Makeda said. She burst out laughing, then sighed.

'Why?' Andrea said.

'Hearing that coming from you of all people. It's what men say: "Come, let me save you from this life. You can move in with me and cook for me and wash my socks." Are you crazy?'

'I'm being serious.'

'You're earning enough for two. And what about the other fourteen? My family in Addis Ababa?'

They had dropped the subject, but Andrea kept asking her what job she had on that evening. She found it bothered her less if she knew. It put it on a different level: a professional one.

On the other hand, it was not that simple at the Love Food dinners. Andrea knew from experience how randy they made you feel. How could Makeda keep a professional distance? And how could Andrea ever mention the incident with Maravan to Makeda? Although they had told each other many intimate things, she had kept quiet about that.

*

A few days after the Staffel and van Genderen dinner, Thevaram and Rathinam were in touch again. They had news for Maravan and asked whether they could come round.

Every previous meeting had cost money. So Maravan took 1,000 francs from behind the Lakshmi shrine and waited for the bell to ring.

The news was a job. Maravan had been asked to cook the Pongal menu for the TCA, the Tamil Cultural Association.

Pongal was the festival in which Tamils offered their thanks for the harvest. An important festival and a nice job.

Thevaram suggested a fee of 1,000 francs, which, of course, Maravan would donate to the good cause. He would then be able to earn money from the commissions that would surely come his way as a result.

Maravan was totally fed up with his sleazy work – one customer had recently called him a sex chef – and the attraction of cooking a normal Tamil celebratory meal for normal Tamil compatriots was so great that he said yes.

'What about Ulagu? Have you heard anything?'

Thevaram and Rathinam exchanged glances. 'Oh yes,' Rathinam said, 'he was rejected.'

'As a soldier?' Maravan's blood raced to his head.

'No, as a Black Tiger.'

When the two had left Maravan put the 1,000 francs behind the shrine again.

*

On a gas ring, rice, lentils, palm sugar and ginger were cooking in a new clay pot, around which fresh turmeric and ginger had been tied. The families were sitting in a semicircle by the cooker. Everybody had new clothes on; the women and girls adorned with flowers were wearing colourful saris or Punjabis.

Suddenly the contents of the pot frothed over the edge, causing the blue gas flame below to flicker yellow.

'*Pongalo Pongal!*' the guests shouted.

Maravan had made the rice pudding, but he could not take part in the boiling-over ceremony. Since the previous day he had been working in the community centre kitchen.

The Tamil Cultural Association had rented and decorated a room there. A few women had been seconded from the Association management to give Maravan a hand. They did it voluntarily, but with little commitment. Given the number of people they were expecting, Maravan had also called up Gnanam, his compatriot who lived above him in the mansard and worked as a kitchen help. He needed someone with experience, so he would have to pay for him out of his own pocket.

The ventilation system in the kitchen worked poorly and the room had no windows. There was a strong smell of lentils, rice, ghee, chilli, cardamom, cinnamon and *hing*, an essential ingredient of many Pongal recipes and a strange herb which only lost its foul smell when cooked, hence its other name: devil's dung.

Maravan cooked four classic vegetarian recipes: *Avial*, a paste made from two different types of lentil, and coconut with *hing* and mixed vegetables. Lemon rice with lentils, mustard seeds, turmeric and *hing*. *Parangikkai puli kuzhambu*, a spicy, sweet-and-sour pumpkin dish with onions, tomatoes and lots of tamarind. *Sakkarai pongal*, a rice pudding with almonds and cashews, lentils, saffron and cardamom.

He was just about to roast the almonds and cashew nuts in a heavy iron frying pan when somebody tapped him on the shoulder. Maravan turned his head with exaggerated haste to show how busy he was and how inopportune the interruption.

Sandana was standing beside him. 'Can I help?'

He thought about it briefly, then handed her his cooking spoon. 'Keep on stirring them around, they mustn't blacken. When they've all turned golden-yellow put them in this bowl and . . . erm . . . call me.'

He hurried to his assistant at the next pot, checked everything was OK, gave a few instructions and moved on to the next.

When he was a child he had seen a Chinese artist in a circus spinning plates on the tops of bendy poles. One to start with, then two, then more until there were about twenty or thirty – he was not so good at counting back then. She had her hands full trying to keep the plates spinning, running between the dancing poles, and always managed to prevent a teetering plate from crashing to the ground at the very last moment.

This is how he felt now as the only chef between a dozen pans, the contents of which could lose their balance at any time.

However, he always spent a bit longer next to Sandana.

33

Pongal is a joyful festival. People look forward to a new beginning and put the past behind them. But here, in the purpose-built community centre on this cold, stormy fourteenth of January 2009, very little of the light-heartedness and confidence that usually accompanied this occasion was palpable.

Almost all those present had family or friends they had to worry about. The Sri Lankan army was at the gates of Mullaitivu, the LTTE was engaged in a fierce fightback, and the civil population was trying in vain to flee.

Many of those at the festival had not been in contact with their relatives for a long time. It was quieter in the hall than in previous years. The faces were more serious and the prayers more ardent.

Maravan had not had any news from his family, either. A rumour was circulating that the shop in Jaffna through which the Batticaoloa Bazaar maintained contact and transferred money had been closed after a raid. It was not the first time; in the past it had always been able to resume its activities after a little bribe. But each time it had taken a few days.

Maravan was sitting at one of the long tables covered with rolls of paper. It was only half full now and the table decoration was askew and full of holes. Some of the guests who had already left had taken flowers with them.

The reason Maravan stayed behind was sitting two tables away, surrounded by parents, aunts, uncles, siblings and friends. Sandana kept looking over at him, but gave no sign he should come and join them.

Several times he had been on the verge of going up to them to ask whether they had enjoyed the meal. He was the chef, after all. That is what chefs do.

But what then? Supposing they said it was nice and thanked him for asking, but did not invite him to sit with them? The thought of standing by their table like a lemon, looking for a way to make a dignified exit, was what kept him at his own table, which was becoming emptier and emptier.

He noticed an argument had started at Sandana's table, an angry exchange of words with her parents. Sandana's eyebrows, which were practically straight, formed a continuous line with the spot above the bridge of her nose.

Now she stood up and, ignoring the calls of her parents, walked to his table.

'Don't look over,' she said, sitting next to him.

Her *pottu*, the spot on the forehead, was still creased by wrinkles of anger.

'An altercation?'

'Culture clash.' She tried to laugh.

'I see.'

'Say something to me. I don't want them to think we've got nothing to say to each other.'

'What do you want me to say?' Maravan realized how stupid

the question was, and added, 'I'm not so good at talking.'

'What are you good at?'

'Cooking.'

'Talk to me about cooking then.'

'I must have been about five when I first watched my great-aunt making *puttu*. She transformed rice and lentils into flour, grated coconut into milk, then worked everything into a dough, and from this made lots of little balls, which she transformed with steam, coconut milk and palm sugar into sweet fake banyan figs. It was then that I learnt that cooking is transformation and nothing more. Cold into warm, hard into soft, sour into sweet. That's why I became a cook. Because I'm fascinated by the process of transformation.'

'You're a wonderful cook.'

'Today was nothing. I'd like to go on from here. Keep on transforming what's already been transformed. Take the thing that's been turned from hard to soft and transform it into something crunchy. Or something foamy. Or something melting. Do you understand? I want . . .' – he searched for the right words – '. . . I want to turn what's familiar into something new. What's expected into something surprising.' He was astonished by his flow of words, and especially by what he was saying. He had never been able to express it so well before.

'We're going now,' a voice said from behind them. Sandana's father had approached their table unnoticed.

'Father, this is Maravan. He did the cooking for all of us today. Maravan, this is my father, Mahit.'

Maravan stood up and made to shake the man's hand. But the latter ignored the gesture, merely repeating, 'We're going now.'

'Fine. I'll come later.'

'No, you're going to come *now*, with us.'

'I'm twenty-two, father.'

'You're coming with us.'

Maravan watched Sandana battling with herself. In the end she raised her shoulders, dropped them again and said, 'Another time, then.' And followed her father.

Maravan was practising making drinks. Not all *Love Menu* diners were content just to have champagne and wine. They asked for cocktails and aperitifs. Maravan's ambition would not allow him to serve mere Camparis or Bloody Marys.

He was currently mixing thick coconut milk with crushed ice, arrack, ginger ale, white tea, *xanthan* and guar. He was going to freeze the pastel-yellow mass for twelve hours at minus twenty degrees, and then serve it on china spoons, together with some pop rocks, as an explosive arrack confection. As with all his alcoholic creations, Andrea would be the guinea pig.

The doorbell rang. Maravan glanced at his watch: almost half past ten at night. He looked through the spyhole – nobody. He picked up the antiquated intercom handset and called out, 'Yes?'

He could detect a woman's voice through the static hissing and crackling. But he could not understand what she was saying. 'Louder, please!' he shouted. Now he was able to make out a word which might have been 'Andrea'. Andrea? At this time? Without having called him first?

He pressed the button to open the door and waited at the entrance to his flat. He could hear soft, rapid steps on the stairs. Then he saw his late guest: Sandana.

She was wearing western clothes: jeans, sweater and the quilted coat he recognized from their first meeting. He thought she looked better in traditional clothes.

He invited her to come in. It was only then that he noticed she was carrying a travel bag. She put it down and greeted him in the Swiss style, with three kisses. It was meant to be totally natural, but she did it rather awkwardly.

'Can I stay the night here?' was the first thing she asked.

He must have looked so surprised that she added, 'On the sofa or the floor, I don't care.'

Maravan knew Hindu Tamil families very well, and he could see an avalanche of consequences ready to descend on him. 'Why aren't you staying at home?'

'I've moved out.'

'I'll give you some money for a hotel.'

'I've got money.'

Maravan recalled her telling him that she worked in a railway travel centre.

Sandana looked at him beseechingly. 'You don't have to sleep with me.'

He smiled. 'Thank God!'

Sandana remained serious. 'But you have to say you did.'

He helped her out of her coat and showed her into the kitchen. 'Just let me finish off what I'm doing here, then you can tell me everything.' He turned the mixer on again, let it run for a few moments, and poured its contents into a flexible form.

'Are you transforming?'

'Yes, coconut schnapps into schnapps coconut.'

For the first time she gave a slight smile.

Maravan put the form into the deep freeze and took Sandana into his living room. When he opened the door, the draught caused the flame of the *deepam* to flicker. Maravan closed the window.

'Sit down, sit down. Would you like some tea? I was just going to make one for myself.'

'Then I'll have one too.' She put her hands together in front of her face, performed a quick bow before Lakshmi, and sat on one of the cushions.

When Maravan returned from the kitchen with the tea, Sandana was sitting exactly as he had left her. He sat down and listened to her story. He could have guessed it.

Some time back Sandana's parents had agreed with the parents of a young man called Padmakar – like her, they were Vaishyas – that the two youngsters should marry. The caste was right, as were the personal histories and the horoscopes. But Sandana did not want to. Now that the wedding was approaching, the quarrel had escalated. The argument that Maravan had witnessed from a distance at Pongal had been about this very matter. And tonight had seen the climax of the drama. She had packed a few things and left. Her mother had cried and her father kept on saying, 'If you go now, don't ever bother coming back.'

'So what now?' Maravan asked when she had reached the end of her tale. She started crying. He watched Sandana for a while, then sat next to her and put his arm around her.

He would have loved to have kissed her, but after what she had just told him this would cause even more problems: she was a Vaishya, he a Shudra. Forget it.

She had stopped crying; she wiped the tears from her eyes and moaned, 'You know I've never been to Sri Lanka.'

'You should be happy about that.'

She gave him a look of astonishment.

'It means you can't be homesick.'

'Aren't you?'

'Always. Sometimes more, sometimes less. But it never goes away completely.'

'Is it really so beautiful there?'

'If you go into the interior on the narrow roads, it's like driving through a single huge village. The roads are lined with trees, and in their shade you can see the houses standing there very secretly, very secure. Sometimes there's a paddy field, then trees and houses again. Sometimes a class of schoolchildren in white uniforms. And then more houses. Sometimes there's more of them, sometimes fewer, but they never stop altogether. Just when you've thought you've seen the last one, the first of a new lot comes into view. One big, inhabited, fertile, tropical park.

'Oh stop! I'm getting homesick.'

*

Sandana slept in Maravan's bed, watched over by his little curry trees. He had made a bed for himself from the cushions where he ate. After giving each other a friendly kiss goodnight, both lay awake for hours, chastely and full of regret.

The following morning Maravan started out of a short, deep sleep. The door to his bedroom was open, the bed was made. On the duvet was a note: *Thanks for everything – S.* And a mobile number.

Her travel bag was still there.

Maravan turned on his computer and went on the internet. He was now checking the LTTE and Sri Lankan government web pages on a regular basis. Neither could be trusted, but if he combined these with reports from the western media and international organizations he could build up an approximate picture of the situation.

The Sri Lankan armed forces had taken Mullaitivu and were pushing further north. The Tamil Tigers would soon be surrounded, as would around 250,000 civilians, according to estimates by the aid organizations. Both sides were accusing each other of using civilians as human shields. In the Swiss media there was little or nothing about the looming humanitarian crisis.

In spite of these chaotic circumstances the Batticaloa Bazaar had begun functioning again as a point of contact. Even before he sat down in front of the screen, Maravan got a call from the Bazaar. He was told he should ring the usual number at eleven the following morning. His sister wanted to speak to him.

Maravan braced himself for bad news.

*

After breakfast he called Sandana. Her phone rang many times before she answered.

'I can't talk at the moment, I've got customers,' she said. 'I'll call you in my break.'

'When is your break?' he asked. But she had already hung up.

So he waited. Waited and thought of the travel bag on the floor beside his mattress, as if it now belonged there.

What was Sandana planning to do? Did she want to risk a scandal and move in with him? And did he want that? He knew of such cases. Of girls who had been born and grew up here, and who refused to conform to the traditions and customs of a country that was alien to them. They accepted the inevitable break with their families and moved in with the men they loved.

Mainly these were men from here. But even in cases where a Tamil woman lived with a Tamil man – especially one from the wrong caste – without the blessing of her parents, the couple would be banished from their families and the community.

Would he want that? Would he want to live with a woman who was excluded from the community? They would have to stay away from all those religious and social occasions or accept the fact that they would be personae non gratae. Could he do that?

If he loved the woman, yes he could.

He pictured Sandana in his mind. Rebellious and resigned, as she had been at the Pongal. Determined and unsure, as she had been yesterday. With her slight Swiss accent when she spoke Tamil. In the jeans and sweater that looked so wrong on her.

Yes, he could.

She finally returned his call.

'You should have woken me. I'd have made you egg hoppers.'

'I looked in on you, but you were in a deep sleep.'

They chatted like lovers after their first night of passion together.

Suddenly she said, 'I've got to go, my break's over. Are you home at lunchtime? I'd like to pick up my bag. I can move in with a colleague of mine.'

34

The time that the owner of the Batticaloa Bazaar had given Maravan was not very handy for Love Food's schedule: eleven in the morning.

They had a job in Falkengässchen, and at that hour Maravan really ought to have been in the kitchen in the middle of his preparations. It had required some organization on his part, and some flexibility from Andrea, to enable him now to be sitting punctually at his computer with headphones and notepad, his heart pounding and hands trembling.

He dialled the number and the connection was instant. The shopkeeper's voice answered. Maravan gave his name and a few seconds later the tear-choked voice of his older sister said, 'Maravan?'

'Has something happened to Ulagu?' he asked.

Hearing sobbing, he waited.

'Nangay,' she uttered.

No, he thought, no, not Nangay. 'What's wrong with her?'

'She's dead,' she stammered. Then only sobs again.

Maravan put his head in his hands and said nothing. Said nothing until he heard his sister's voice, now clearer and more composed. 'Brother, are you there?'

'How?' he asked.

'Her heart. One moment she was alive and the next she was dead.'

'But her heart was so strong.'

After a pause, Maravan's sister said, 'Her heart was weak. She had a heart attack two years ago.'

'Why didn't you tell me?'

'She didn't want you to know.'

'Why not?'

'She was afraid you might come back.'

When Maravan had finished talking to his sister he went into the bedroom, took Nangay's photo from the wall and placed it by the domestic shrine. Then he kneeled and said a prayer for her. Was Nangay right? Would he have gone back if he had known about her heart attack?

Probably not.

That evening Maravan varied the *Love Menu*. He cooked all the dishes exactly in the way Nangay had shown him.

He did not prepare the *urad* lentil purée marinated in sugared milk as 'man and woman', but dried it in portions in the oven.

The mixture of saffron, milk and almonds he simply served as a warm drink. And he made a paste out of the saffron ghee, which was eaten with warm milk.

He used neither the rotary evaporator nor jellification, and made no attempt to defamiliarize textures or aromas.

The meal that evening was a homage to the woman to whom he owed everything. Just for tonight, he did not want to abuse her art for something she would never have approved of.

All the while, curry leaves and cinnamon bark sat in hot coconut oil, filling the whole apartment with the aroma of his childhood. In memory of Nangay.

Andrea had noticed instantly that something was wrong. Maravan did not turn up until late into their preparation time. When he finally arrived, the whole apartment was soon smelling more strongly of curry than his obsessively aired kitchens ever had in the past. And what she served up had nothing to do with the *Love Menu* she knew.

Right at the start she had made a comment about the changes and received an angry glare in return. 'Like this or not at all,' was all he had uttered, and throughout the remainder of the afternoon and evening he only spoke when necessary, to discuss timings.

The client – a regular – was visibly disappointed when she brought the 'greeting from the kitchen'. It was a small spoon with a dark paste next to a shot glass of hot milk, which she had to announce as '*urad* lentils in hot milk'. But the woman he had booked for the evening was new and so excited that he did not let it show.

Shortly before Andrea left the apartment – Maravan had gone long before, almost without saying goodbye – the client, wrapped in a Turkish towel, came out of the room, handed her three 200 franc notes and grinned: 'At first I thought it was the alternative version of the menu. But I must say, it got me going even more. Compliments to the chef.'

35

Once again Maravan had spent more than two hours in Dr Kerner's waiting room. The well-thumbed newspapers lying around all carried the same lead story: the forthcoming swearing-in of the first black president of the United States, Barack Hussein Obama.

This event was also the main topic of conversation among those waiting. The Tamils were hoping for a Sri Lanka policy that was less government-friendly, the Iraqis for a rapid withdrawal of American troops from their country, and the Africans for greater engagement in Zimbabwe and Darfur.

When Maravan was finally called into the surgery, Dr Kerner looked up from his patient file and asked, 'How's your great-aunt?'

'She's dead.'

'I'm very sorry to hear that. You did all you could. Why have you come to see me?'

'It's not me. It's about my great-aunt. You asked me last time whether her heart was OK. Why?'

'If she'd been suffering from certain circulation problems she should not have taken the Minirin. It works as a blood-thinner. It cancels out the effects of anticoagulants and so could bring about a stroke or a heart attack. How did she die?'

'From a heart attack.'

'And now you're worried the medicine may have been to blame. Not very likely. She would have had to have had a pre-history of circulation problems.'

'She had a heart attack. Two years ago.'

Now Dr Kerner cast him a look of mild horror. 'You should have told me.'

'I didn't know. She kept it to herself.'

36

Towards the end of January a small piece of business news caused astonishment in professional circles. It even found its way into the daily papers.

Kugag, the firm defying the economic crisis by manufacturing in the renewable energy sector, had announced it had entered into a joint venture with hoogteco, a Dutch company, the biggest European supplier of solar and wind energy – and Kugag's biggest competitor.

All who knew – and some commentators did know – just how rapidly developments progressed in this area, and how sensitive technological knowledge in the sector was, were amazed by this move. Because it could not occur without sharing know-how.

Experts asked openly what Kugag, the smaller but more dynamic of the two firms, would gain from this collaboration. It was considered to have one of the leading research departments in the world; its production capacity had recently expanded to meet future demand; its order book was full and analysts knew of some promising product innovations that were in the pipeline.

Kugag did not have any image problems either. Its CEO had recently been chosen as manager of the year in the 'new technology' sector.

If anybody was going to profit from this deal it could only be hoogteco.

Hans Staffel, Kugag's CEO and normally a good communicator, raised eyebrows on this occasion with his botched information policy. It was hoogteco that went public with the news. To begin with, Kugag refused to make any comment, then announced that the matter was not yet definite, and very belatedly issued a terse communiqué that confirmed everything stated in the Dutch report.

On the following Monday, Kugag was hit hard on the stock exchange. By contrast, hoogteco had an outstanding start to the week.

A spokeswoman for Kugag – the firm had hired a spokeswoman, no doubt on the advice of its communications consultant – played this down and described the deal as a completely normal, very specific business venture, entered into from a position of strength.

One commentator expressed doubt at this strength and wondered about possible financial difficulties that may have resulted from speculation on the American sub-prime market.

Another commentator wondered why the board had not prevented this development. Or whether Staffel had not exceeded his authority here.

There was no reaction forthcoming from the CEO himself, who usually did not shy away from the public eye.

February 2009

37

Maravan was busy most evenings at the moment. But he was able to interrupt his preparations at lunchtime, when he met Sandana. He waited for her outside the travel centre and then they would go to a café, restaurant or snack bar at the station.

They would use this scant hour to tell each other about their respective lives.

Once she asked, 'If we were in Sri Lanka now, what do you think we'd be doing?'

'You mean now? Right now?'

Sandana nodded. 'At half past twelve.'

'Local time?'

'Local time.'

'It would be hot, but it wouldn't be raining.'

'So, what are we doing?'

'We're on the beach. It's a little cooler in the sea breeze under the palm trees. The sea is calm. It's generally calm in February.'

'Are we alone?'

'Nobody to be seen for miles.'

'Why are we in the shade and not in the water?'

'We don't have our swimming costumes. Only our sarongs.'

'You can go in the water with those on.'

'But they'd become see-through.'

'Would that bother you?'

'Looking at you? No.'

'Let's go in then.'

On another occasion Maravan told her about his fears for Ugalu. And about Nangay. What she had meant to him. And that he felt partly to blame for her death.

'Didn't you say she would have dehydrated without the medicine?'

Maravan nodded.

'And didn't your sister say, "One moment she was alive and the next she was dead"?'

They became closer. They rarely touched physically, although they gave each other the hello and goodbye kisses that were normal in this city, although improper in their culture.

She was still sharing a flat with her workmate, a jolly woman from the Berner Oberland, who he had once met when the two of them were leaving the travel centre at the same time. Sandana had no contact with her parents.

One evening in February, Maravan, who had been cooking in Falkengässchen and was able to clock off early, was sitting at his computer surfing the internet. The news from his country was getting more and more depressing.

The army had established a safety zone for refugees, which, according to matching reports from the LTTE and various aid organizations, they were now bombarding. There were many civilian deaths. Whoever was able to flee the conflict zone was doing so, and being immediately interned in refugee camps. Many people were saying that the government forces were on the brink of victory. Maravan and most of his compatriots knew that a victory was not the way forward to peace.

Shortly after eleven o'clock that night there was an insistent ringing at his door.

Through the spyhole he could see a middle-aged Tamil man.

'What do you want?' Maravan asked when the man took his finger off the bell for a moment.

'Open the door!' the man ordered.

'Who are you?'

'Her father. Now open the door or I'll kick it in!'

Maravan opened the door. He now recognized Sandana's father, who stormed into the flat.

'Where is she?'

'If you're talking about Sandana, she's not here.'

'Of course she's here.'

With a gesture of his hand Maravan invited him to take a look around. Mahit inspected every room, went into the bathroom and even looked on the balcony.

'Where is she?'

'At home, I expect.'

'She hasn't been at home for a long time now!'

'I think she's staying with a friend.'

'Ha! Friend! She's living here!'

'Is that what she told you?'

'We don't talk any more!' He was practically shouting. Then he suddenly calmed down and repeated at normal volume, 'We don't talk any more.' He sounded astonished, as if he had only become aware of this fact just now.

Maravan could see tears welling up in the man's eyes. He put a hand on his shoulder. The man angrily shook it off.

'Sit down. I'll make you some tea.' He pointed to the chair by his monitor. Mahit sat obediently and put his head in his hands, sobbing gently.

When Maravan brought the tea, Sandana's father had composed himself. He thanked Maravan and took small sips.

'Why does she want us to think she's living here when she's staying with a friend?'

'She doesn't want to marry the man you've chosen for her.'

Mahit shook his head in puzzlement. 'But he's a good man. My wife and I spent a long time finding him. It wasn't easy.'

'Women here want to be able to find their own husbands.'

Mahit flared up again. 'She's not from here!'

'But not from there, either.'

The father nodded and started crying again. This time he made no attempt to wipe away his tears. 'This bloody war. This shitty, bloody war,' he sobbed.

When he had calmed down, he finished his tea, apologized and left.

38

Maravan was no longer quite so focused as before. Now, almost every lunchtime he went out for an hour, whereas in the past he would have been busy concentrating on preparing dinner.

'Just popping out for a bite,' he would say.

When he returned he was usually quite cheerful, which he had not been for a long time, ever since that evening when he cooked the alternative menu.

Not long afterwards the client had ordered the same menu again and a different woman, but Maravan had refused outright.

'It's not meant for that,' he told Andrea.

'But the client says it worked brilliantly.' 'That wasn't the intention,' was Maravan's answer. And with that he considered the matter closed.

He would not explain what the issue was, and she did not probe him. It was a delicate topic. She did not want to upset him. She was happy that he seemed so jolly lately.

It was only by chance that she discovered the reason for the change in his behaviour. Makeda had a booking with someone attending a UN conference in Geneva, and so Andrea had taken her to the station. After the train left she went into a sandwich bar on the station concourse. And it was there that she saw him.

Maravan was sitting at a small table with a pretty Tamil woman. They had eyes and ears only for each other.

Andrea hesitated for a moment, but then decided she would disturb their idyll after all. She went up to the table and said, 'I hate to interrupt.'

The girl looked enquiringly, first at her then at Maravan. He had lost his tongue.

'I'm Andrea, Maravan's business partner.' She offered her hand and the young woman took it with a relieved smile.

'And I'm Sandana.' She spoke Swiss dialect without a hint of an accent.

As Maravan did not invite her to sit down with them, Andrea left soon afterwards, saying 'See you later' to Maravan, and 'Pleased to have met you' to Sandana.

Later, in Falkengässchen, she said, 'Why don't you take the poor girl to a nicer restaurant?'

'She works in the travel centre and only has a short lunch break.'

Andrea smiled. 'Now it's all making sense: you're in love.'

Maravan did not look up from his work. He just shook his head and muttered, 'I'm not.'

'Well, she is,' was Andrea's reply.

The following morning another piece of Kugag-related business news caught the media's attention. Hans Staffel, one of the Managers of the Year, had been relieved of all duties with immediate effect. 'Due to differences of opinion regarding the firm's strategic orientation.' The commentators thought it was obvious: the CEO's dismissal was connected to his opaque decision to enter a joint venture with one of the company's largest competitors.

'Look! We know him,' Makeda said, showing Andrea the official portrait which Staffel had got an expensive photographer to produce for the annual report during happier times. Andrea was leafing through the newspapers she had bought while fetching the breakfast croissants. Makeda was watching her; she could not read German.

'What's happened to him?'

Andrea read the article. 'Booted out.'

'But I thought he was so brilliant.'

'He screwed things up by getting involved with a Dutch firm.'

'Wasn't the guy he came to Falkengässchen with one of those?'

'What?'

'A Dutchman.'

Maravan was reading the paper for another reason. More than 10,000 of his compatriots had held a demonstration outside the UN building in Geneva. They were demanding an immediate end to the military offensive.

Over the last few days the news from Sri Lanka was getting ever more catastrophic. The area occupied by the LTTE had shrunk to an enclave of no more than 150 square kilometres, in the middle of which stood the town of Puthukkudiyiruppu. Kilinochchi, the Elephant Pass, and the ports of Mullaitivu and Chalai were in government hands. The Red Cross estimated that besides the roughly 10,000 LTTE soldiers, a further 250,000 people were surrounded and coming repeatedly under fire.

While demonstrations were taking place in Geneva, the government in Colombo was celebrating the sixty-first anniversary of Sri Lankan independence with a military parade. 'I am confident the Tigers will be completely defeated within a few days,' President Mahinda Rajapaksa declared. He called on all Sri Lankans who had left the country because of the war to return.

The Government had published not very convincing photographs of a two-storeyed, comfortable-looking bunker that had housed the Tamil commandant Prabhakaran, but from where he had made a hasty departure. A rumour was circulating that he had left the country.

It was not until he put down the paper that Maravan noticed the picture of a man he had let into the apartment in Falkengässchen the previous month, because Andrea had been out buying matches. All he read was the caption: *Fired: Manager of the Year Hans Staffel.*

Later that morning, when they were still in bed, Makeda said out of the blue, 'He took photos of him.'

'Who did?'

'The Dutch guy. When the bloke who's got the sack went into the next-door room with Cécile. After a while the Dutch guy stood up, took something from his jacket, opened the door quietly and stayed there until Cécile sent him out.'

'How do you know he took pictures?'

'Cécile shouted out, "*Ça suffit!* Photos cost extra!"'

39

Just for a change, Love Food cooked for a married couple again. The clients were regulars with Esther Dubois, the sex therapist – a sort of arty-crafty couple in their mid-forties who were working very seriously at their relationship. Andrea had no idea where they had got her details from. She suspected they were being passed around by word of mouth among Esther Dubois's patients, because more and more clients were coming from this source.

They lived in a house with a vegetable garden and the wife wanted Maravan to swear that he would use only organic ingredients. Maravan agreed, although he could not provide a cast-iron guarantee for all the molecular texturizers.

While they were making their preparations, Andrea said, 'Did you hear Staffel got the sack?'

'The crisis is sparing nobody.'

'Makeda said the Dutchman took photos of him while he was shagging.'

'I don't want to know what they do behind those doors.'

'Don't you see? He photographed him shagging and blackmailed him with the pictures. He's supposed to have made some pretty strange business decisions all of a sudden, and then started working on something together with a competitor.'

Maravan reacted with a shrug.

'And guess what nationality these competitors are?'

'Dutch?' Maravan guessed.

Maravan was not the only one in love. For the first time in years – how many he could not remember – Dalmann had lost his sick heart, too. It was now in the possession of someone who had little use for it: Makeda, a call girl from Ethiopia and constant companion of Andrea, CEO of Love Food.

He booked her several evenings a week. Not because his sexual appetite was insatiable or his performance in bed impressive; on this matter Dalmann was well aware of his age, his heart and the daily cocktail of medicines. No, he simply felt fantastic in her company. He loved her sense of humour and her sometimes obscure irony. But most of all, he could not get enough of her.

For a large sum of money, therefore, he led an almost conventional relationship with Makeda in his house, watching television and spending hours losing to her at backgammon.

Unlike other girlfriends in the past, she never demanded to be seen in public with him. She was in no doubt that theirs was a purely business relationship.

To begin with he had liked that, but as time went on it bothered him. He would ask whether she liked him just a little bit, and each time she would give him the same answer: 'Like you a little bit? I absolutely worship you.'

Because she was non-committal he would give her presents. A pearl necklace, a matching pearl bracelet and a midnight-black mink stole.

He even took her to the Huwyler one evening.

Makeda ate her way through the *Menu Surprise* as if she dined like that every day. And she stuck to champagne all evening, which pained the chef in Huwyler, but pleased the businessman in him. Dalmann still drank wine after the aperitif, leaving the choice to the sommelier.

Word got around the kitchen that evening that Dalmann had a sensational companion. The entire team, one by one, peeked at his table from the serving counter and gave their opinion: dancer, model or tart.

Makeda was a luxury that, strictly speaking, Dalmann could not afford. Shares in the largest bank, where his supposedly safe investments had been made, had not recovered at all. Quite the opposite, in fact. The bank, which was being propped up by the state, had just announced a loss of 20 billion francs – a loss never seen before in the country's economic history. Customers had withdrawn 226 billion francs, and shares had lost almost two thirds of their value over this period. In addition, the American tax authorities were threatening to revoke the bank's licence if it did not hand over the data relating to a few hundred US citizens suspected of tax evasion. Without a licence in the United States, the largest Swiss bank might as well shut up shop.

On the other hand, the business with Staffel and van Genderen had taken a positive turn. Although the new management, under pressure from shareholders, was desperately trying to rescind the deal between Kugag and hoogteco, he no longer cared as his commission had been paid, and to the right bank.

He was amazed how quickly van Genderen had talked poor old Staffel round; he had no idea how he had managed it. He did have a suspicion, though. The rumour (spread by a gossip columnist for the big daily paper) that Staffel's wife had filed for divorce gave some indication. Not Dalmann's problem either.

In a different field, the intermediary and consultancy work was also going beautifully well. That is to say, the business involving his Thai and Pakistani contacts, Waen and Fajahat. The two men had reached an agreement with Carlisle, the products had been sold to the United States and then delivered to Thailand and Pakistan. Dalmann doubted they were still in these countries. Most likely the Thai consignment had made its way unofficially to the Bay of Bengal and been loaded on to LTTE ships; the Pakistani one had probably been shipped officially to Colombo.

Of course, all that was beyond Dalmann's responsibility. All he had done, and perfectly legally too, was offer up his services and receive an appropriate commission. If he hadn't done it, somebody else would. This fee had also been deposited at a smaller, but more solid bank.

This supplementary income did not make him rich, but it made his luxuries seem less ill-advised.

40

At about nine o'clock in the evening two small aeroplanes flew from the north towards Colombo. The cockpits were manned by the two Black Air Tigers Col. Rooban and Lt. Col. Siriththiran. They had taken off from a street in the encircled war zone. Rooban had left behind a letter in which he implored the young people to join the Liberation Tigers.

They parted company shortly before reaching the capital. One of the planes flew towards the airbase at Katunayake; the other's target was the air force command centre in the middle of Colombo.

At 9.20 there was a blackout in Colombo. A few sirens were audible.

Maravan was in a Tamil grocer's when the news came through. The sound of whooping and clapping suddenly erupted from a room at the back. The owner came into the shop and bellowed, 'We've bombed Katunayake and Colombo! We haven't lost yet!'

Maravan had picked up some *sali* rice, long pepper and palm sugar, and was waiting to pay by the cash till. But customers and staff were jabbering away wildly to each other. Katunayake and Colombo! Bombed! And the army's forever saying the Tigers have been conquered! We haven't lost yet!

Maravan went over to the shopkeeper. 'Completely defeated, Rajapaksa said, completely defeated!' he yelled, his voice cracking.

'Could I pay, please?' Maravan said.

'And they said Prabhakaran had left the country! Not a trace of him. There's a photo of him with the two pilots on the internet! Ha!'

'Could I pay, please?'

'Aren't you happy?'

'I'll be happy when there's peace.'

The following day Maravan experimented late into the night burning cinnamon bark in his smoker. When he opened the kitchen balcony door to let fresh air in again, he could hear cheering and clapping above him. He went onto the balcony and looked up at the window.

On the kitchen balcony of the flat next to his stood Murugan, a husband and father who smoked on the balcony. He was also looking up.

'Another air attack?' Maravan asked.

'*Slumdog Millionaire*.'

'Slumdog millionaire?'

'A film about a young man from Mumbai who lives in the slums and wins a million on a TV gameshow. It's cleaning up at the Oscars. And the Ratnams are cheering every time.'

'But the Ratnams aren't Indians, are they?'

'More Indian than Swiss, like all of us.'

*

Dalmann was concerned with neither the events in and around Sri Lanka nor the Oscar ceremony. He was a man of business and this, dear God, was providing plenty of excitement in itself.

His bank, for whose recovery he sent prayers to heaven every night, had begged the Government's permission to release the customer details of 300 American citizens accused of tax evasion. This was the nail in the coffin of bank secrecy.

Saab, the Swedish car manufacturer belonging to the ailing General Motors, was bankrupt. Not that this surprised Dalmann – he had never had much time for these four-wheeled understatements for intellectuals – but the fact that the Government had allowed it to happen made him think.

Germany had announced an economic stimulus package of 50 billion euros and pushed up new borrowing to record levels.

And now this.

Schaeffer arrived while he was still in bed, where he would love to have wallowed a while longer in Makeda's scent.

Dalmann kept him waiting for an hour, then came into the breakfast room showered, shaved and rather too perfumed. His colleague was sitting with a cup of tea and two garlands of apple peel.

'What's so urgent?' was Dalmann's greeting. He could sense this was no small matter.

'The anti-arms export crowd.'

'What's that got to do with me?'

'They've tracked down Waen.'

'And?'

'They were given a tip-off that he'd bought armoured howitzers that had been returned to the US.'

'You know as well as I do there's nothing illegal about that.'

'But they've found out he's supplying them to the Tamil Tigers.'

'That's his problem.'

'I'm glad you seem so relaxed about it.'

'And you're not?'

'They'll publish it in one of their leaflets, one of our journalist friends with a good nose for a story will dig around and it's not impossible they'll come up with your name.'

'In connection with Waen?'

'In connection with Carlisle. You helped arrange his acquisition.'

'So what?' Dalmann sounded unperturbed. But they both knew he could not afford to be named in connection with such a deal.

Schaeffer got up. 'I just wanted to warn you.'

'Wait, not so fast.'

Schaeffer sat again.

'What can we do?'

'Not a great deal.'

'But a little?'

Schaeffer pretended to consider this long and hard. 'We could perhaps ensure the publication taking the lead in this matter is one over which we could exert a modicum of influence.'

Dalmann nodded. There was only one such paper. 'How do you plan to arrange it?'

'I'll give them the tip-off about Carlisle. On the condition they keep you out of it.'

The man was good. He got on your nerves, but he was good. 'And how are you going to prevent another journalist from researching the story?'

'Journalists don't research their colleagues' exposés. They copy them.'

Schaeffer said goodbye and Dalmann set about his breakfast feeling somewhat reassured.

41

Shortly before eleven o'clock in the morning Andrea rang the bell beside the 'M' in the block of flats where Makeda lived. She had been waiting for her in vain all night. Although Makeda had said Dalmann had booked her, it rarely lasted all night.

One of their agreements was that neither of them should ever wait for the other, or ever expect them to come for sure. It should always be a happy surprise when they visited each other. But between them, as between all lovers, there were many agreements. And like all lovers, sometimes they did not stick to them.

Something else they had agreed was to ask no questions. They wanted to be able to keep secrets from each other. Not big ones. Just things that were no business of the other person.

Andrea could not always manage this, however. She never asked directly, but occasionally she would say, more to herself than Makeda, 'Do I really want to know what you've been up to all night?'

Makeda never answered these rhetorical questions. And she never put one to Andrea either.

Makeda's sleepy voice sounded over the intercom. 'Yessss?'

'It's me, Andrea.'

Makeda pressed the button to open the door, and when the lift arrived at the fourth floor she was waiting for Andrea in the doorway.

Andrea greeted her with a fleeting kiss and went in.

'Coffee?' Makeda asked.

Andrea had been livid, but now that she saw her girlfriend standing there, so beautiful, so gracious, so relaxed, her anger dissipated.

'Why not?' she said, returning Makeda's smile.

Makeda made two espressos, put them down on the small table between the armchairs, sat opposite Andrea, and crossed her legs. 'Dalmann,' she said with a dismissive wave of her hand.

'All a bit much' – Andrea copied the gesture – 'Dalmann. In my opinion.'

'He pays well and isn't hard work.'

'He's a nasty old bugger who does dodgy business deals. He organized that evening with the Dutchman and the manager when the photos were taken.'

'How do you know?'

'The Dutch guy was accompanied by Dalmann's dogsbody.'

'Schaeffer? Interesting.'

'I know this goes against our arrangement, but I really hate the way you spend so much time with Dalmann. He disgusts me.'

'It's my job to spend time with men who disgust other women.'

'There are plenty of others.'

'He's one of Kull's best clients. Good for business, he says.'

Andrea made an unhappy face. 'Oh Makeda,' she sighed, 'it's so hard.'

Makeda took pity on her. 'I've never fucked him.'

Andrea waited for her to continue.

'He can't. He's got a weak heart. He swallows thousands of pills every day. And drinks like a fish, too.'

'So what do you do then?'

'Question not allowed.'

'I know. So, what?'

'Talk, eat, watch telly. Like an old married couple.'

'And that's it?'

Makeda laughed. 'Sometimes he wants to watch me getting undressed. And I have to pretend I haven't noticed. He's a voyeur.'

'Disgusting.'

'Oh, come on. It's easy money.'

Andrea stood up, went over to Makeda and gave her a passionate kiss.

42

The weekly review *Freitag* had taken the report by the opponents to the arms exports and exposed the deal involving the decommissioned armed howitzers.

Next to pictures of the howitzers and a diagram of the Bay of Bengal, photos of the American businessman, Carlisle, and his Thai counterpart, Waen, appeared prominently in the report. Details about the two men were sparse, but readers learnt the following. On behalf of the manufacturer – and perfectly legally – Carlisle had acquired the howitzers for next to nothing from the authorities responsible for scrapping or returning them to the country of manufacture. Via the United States he had sold them on to the Thai, Waen, no doubt at a massive profit. Waen had then conveyed them to his country.

This is where the trail of the M109s came to a halt, but it was suspected they had been resold and stored on one of the 'floating warehouses', as the ships were called which supplied their customers in the Bay of Bengal. Until the recent fall of the ports Mullaitivu and Chalai, the main customers had been the LTTE.

Satisfied, Dalmann put *Freitag* beside his breakfast plate and picked up the daily paper. The previous day, just before the first PE lesson, the roof of a sports hall in St Gallen had collapsed under the weight of snow. Nobody had been injured.

*

Sandana was sitting at counter twelve. Andrea had not recognized her at first glance in her work blouse and the rather stuffy shawl that went with it.

Sitting on the chairs in the travel centre were people waiting with their tickets. They looked up every time there was a buzz and the numbers on the display board changed.

Andrea had taken several non-consecutive tickets, in case she was sent to the wrong counter.

Once again it was her habit of interfering in other people's lives that had brought her here. Makeda wanted to cook her an Ethiopian dinner when she had an evening off, and had casually mentioned they could also invite Maravan and his girlfriend.

Andrea liked the idea, but was almost certain Maravan would say no. First, because he still refused to call Sandana his girlfriend; and second, because the only reason he did not frown at Andrea's relationship with Makeda was because he ignored it.

Maravan was becoming depressed by the situation in Sri Lanka. But Andrea also suspected things were not running smoothly with Sandana. And his career as a 'sex chef', as he sometimes referred to it bitterly, did not make him happy either.

A dinner with the four of them might help improve the working atmosphere.

She had come here, therefore, to pre-empt Maravan. She wanted to invite Sandana and then present him with a fait accompli.

The very first of her numbers was for counter twelve. Sandana recognized her and even remembered her name. 'How can I help you?'

'It's a private matter,' Andrea said. 'My girlfriend's cooking an Ethiopian dinner tomorrow night and I'd love it if you and Maravan could come over.'

Sandana was slightly flummoxed.

'Please come.'

'Does Maravan want me to?'

Andrea did not hesitate for a moment. 'Yes.'

'Then I'd love to.'

'Looking forward to it.'

That afternoon the troughs of 'Emma', the winter storm, had moved across the country. An occasional gust of wind made the candles flicker in Andrea's spacious flat. They were sitting around the dining table; Makeda and Andrea were smoking, Sandana and Maravan drinking tea. They were in that relaxed and cheerful mood a good meal can create.

It was an elegant gathering at Andrea's that evening. Makeda was wearing a floor-length embroidered *tibeb*, Sandana a light-blue sari, Andrea a low-cut evening dress, and Maravan had surprised everybody with his suit and tie.

He had declined Andrea's invitation without hesitation.

'Shame,' she said. 'Sandana's coming.'

'I find that hard to believe. Sandana is a decent Tamil girl.'

Andrea smiled. 'Then it might be smarter if you accompanied her.'

So far he had not regretted coming. He had enjoyed the meal. It was not so different from the food in his country. Spicy and made with onions, garlic, ginger, cardamom, cloves, turmeric, fenugreek, cumin, chilli, nutmeg and cinnamon.

Makeda had cooked with ghee, too. Except it was spiced and called *niter kibbeh*.

And they had also eaten without cutlery. Even without crockery. The table which had been covered with white paper was laid out with *injeras*, large flat sourdough breads made from teff, a variety of millet that these days was farmed almost exclusively in Ethiopia. The dishes were put straight onto the breads, and guests would tear pieces off and roll them up as if they were making large edible joints.

'Sometimes we make a single *injera*, as large as a tablecloth. But you can't do it with the stoves here.'

The company was also good. None of Maravan's fears had materialized. Sandana had not been shocked by the fact that the hosts were a couple, or by Makeda's profession, which did not remain a secret for long. The three women were very much at ease with each other, like old friends. Maravan relaxed.

Sandana's liberal attitude had also helped him to discard his reservations about Makeda. The dinner had done its bit, too. Anybody who could cook like that could not be so bad after all.

But at some point the women hit upon a subject which made Maravan feel tense again.

'Maravan tells me that in your culture it's the parents who decide who you marry.' Andrea had asked the question.

'Unfortunately,' Sandana sighed.

'So how do your parents find the right man?' Makeda asked.

'Through relatives, friends; sometimes they use specialist agencies, sometimes they use the internet. And when they've found a contender the horoscope has to be right, and the caste and so on.'

'And love?'

'Love is seen as an unreliable matchmaker.'

'What about you two?' Makeda asked.

Sandana looked at Maravan, who was scrutinizing the patch of table in front of him. She shook her head.

A gust of wind shook the window, slightly ruffling the curtain.

'But here you can marry whoever you like,' Andrea declared.

'Fine. If you don't care about giving your family a bad name and ruining the chances of your siblings marrying.' After a brief pause Sandana added, 'And breaking your parents' hearts.'

'How about your own heart?' Andrea asked.

'That comes second.'

For a short while the only sound was the distant slamming of a shutter that the wind was toying with. Then Makeda asked, 'What about you? How come you were able to leave home?'

Now Sandana lowered her eyes too. Then she said softly, 'In my case the heart doesn't come second.'

In the embarrassing silence that followed Makeda said cheerily, 'Well, you don't have to be married to jump into bed with each other.'

'Then you'd better not get caught. That's just as bad as marrying outside of your caste. It brings shame to the entire family. Even to those who are back in Sri Lanka.' After a brief pause, Sandana added bitterly, 'But if it goes on like this, soon there won't be anyone left to bring shame to.'

'More tea or anything else?' Andrea asked cheerfully.

Maravan gave Sandana an enquiring look. If she said yes, he would have another one, too.

But Sandana did not say yes or no. She said something unexpected: 'Nobody writes anything about this war, there's nothing on telly about this war, the politicians don't talk about this war, and quite clearly this war is not a suitable topic for dinner party conversation!'

Sandana had sat bolt upright in her chair and knitted her beautiful eyebrows. Maravan placed a hand on her shoulder and Andrea wore a guilty expression.

'It's a Third World war,' Makeda said. 'I was also driven out by a Third World war that people pretended wasn't happening. These days Third World wars aren't an issue for the First World.'

'But they are good business.' Sandana grabbed her handbag, which was hanging from the back of her chair, briefly rummaged in it and brought out a folded piece of paper. It was the article about the 'Scrap connection' which she had torn out of *Freitag*.

'Here.' She gave it to Andrea. 'They're happy to sell scrap tanks to Sri Lanka using a roundabout route. But they don't believe the people fleeing the war are in danger.'

Andrea started reading the article; her girlfriend looked over her shoulder.

'I know them,' Makeda said, pointing to the photographs of Waen and Carlisle.

Andrea and Sandana stared at her in astonishment. 'Those guys? How?' Andrea asked.

Makeda rolled her eyes. 'I'll give you three guesses.'

Maravan stood up and went round to look at the slightly tattered piece of paper. Andrea flattened it out with her hands and Makeda switched on the light above the table. An oriental man with glasses and a beefy American stared back at them.

'I'm absolutely certain. And do you know who arranged the date?' Makeda did not wait for anyone to guess. 'Dalmann and Schaeffer.'

'I'm really sorry I behaved badly,' Sandana said. They were standing under a tram shelter on line 12. Sandana had to change here; Maravan had broken his journey to wait with her. It was cold and gusts of wind were still raging.

'You didn't behave badly. You were right.'

'Who are Dalmann and Schaeffer?'

'Clients.'

'Yours or Makeda's?'

'Both.'

'Why do you call yourselves Love Food?'

Makeda and Andrea had used the name all evening long, as if it were a brand everybody knew, like McDonald's or Mövenpick. He wondered why Sandana had not asked this question during the dinner itself. 'It's a good name,' he replied.

Sandana smiled. 'Come on, Maravan, tell me.'

He looked in the direction where her tram would come from. Nothing. 'Well, er . . . I cook these dinners that . . .' – he searched for the right word – '. . . stimulate.'

'Stimulate the appetite?'

Maravan did not know whether she was pulling his leg. 'Sort of, yes,' he answered, embarrassed.

'Where did you learn that?'

'From Nangay. Everything from Nangay.'

A gust of wind swept through the newspaper box, fluttering the handful of free newspapers still in it.

When she got on her tram, Sandana gave him a shy kiss on the mouth. Before the door shut she said, 'Will you cook me something too one day?'

Maravan nodded, smiling. The tram left. Sandana stood right at the back and waved to him.

March 2009

43

It was thanks to an unnamed source that *Freitag* had come across Jafar Fajahat. Its latest edition told readers of the odyssey of some disused armoured personnel carriers via the United States to Pakistan, the biggest arms supplier to the Sri Lankan army.

The article again published photographs of Steven X, Carlisle and Waen. What was new was a portrait of a moustachioed Pakistani called Kazi Razzaq. *Freitag* reported that he came from the entourage of Jafar Fajahat, which had played a central role in the nuclear smuggling affair.

The captions were fairly sensational: *Supplying the Liberation Tigers: Waen. Supplying the Army: Razzaq. Supplying Both: Carlisle.*

'Let's hope it pans out well,' Dalmann groaned when Schaeffer brought him the newspaper.

And it did pan out well. Although the daily press picked up the report and it was circulated in the electronic media as well, nobody seemed to be interested in delving any deeper into the matter.

The other news also worked slightly in Dalmann's favour. In the American state of Alabama a man went on a killing spree, shooting dead eleven people, including his mother, then turned the gun on himself.

The following day a seventeen-year-old boy in Winnenden, a suburb of Stuttgart, shot dead twelve people at his former school, including three passers-by, and finished by shooting himself.

And then the day after that the Swiss government accepted the OECD standard, which signalled the end of bank secrecy, as Dalmann had predicted.

The relocation of some scrap munitions to a war zone pretty much neglected by the media had lost a lot of its newsworthiness.

They met at the rearmost covered bench on platform 8. Sandana had suggested this meeting point; she said she wanted to talk without being disturbed. She also sorted out their lunch: for each of them two pretzel rolls – one cheese, the other ham – a bottle of still mineral water and an apple.

Maravan was there first. A little further along the platform, where the roof finished, the asphalt was shining wet. A light but persistent rain had been falling since the previous night.

There were a lot of passengers on the other side of the tracks, but on his side the platform was empty. The last train had just left; the next would not be arriving for a while. Sandana had left nothing to chance.

Now she arrived, wearing trousers, railway uniform and quilted coat. Maravan got up from the bench; they greeted each other with their usual kisses and sat down.

He gave her a sideways glance. He recognized her expression from the Pongal: rebellious and resigned. She passed him the latest edition of *Freitag*. 'Page twelve,' was all she said.

Maravan read the article and studied the photograph of Kazi Razzaq next to the now familiar ones of Waen and Carlisle. When he had finished he looked at Sandana, who had been watching him expectantly.

'Well?' she asked.

'Arms smugglers,' he replied with a shrug. 'They simply don't operate according to moral principles.'

'Yes, I know that, too. But chefs. Chefs should watch out who they're cooking for.'

It was only now that he realized what she was getting at. 'You mean because of this Dalmann chap?'

Sandana gave a resolute nod of the head. 'If he's involved with the American and Thai man, then he must have something to do with the Pakistani as well.'

Maravan shrugged again, slightly at a loss. 'I suppose it's possible.'

Sandana gave him a look of disbelief. 'Is that all? The man's involved with individuals who supply the arms that our people are killing each other with, and you cook for him?'

'I didn't know.'

'And now you do?'

Maravan thought about it. 'I'm a chef,' he replied eventually.

'Chefs have consciences too.'

'A conscience doesn't pay the bills.'

'But you can't sell it either.'

'Do you know what I do with the money?' Maravan now sounded tetchy. 'I support my family and the fight for liberation.'

'So with the money from the arms smugglers you're supporting the fight for liberation. Great.'

He stood and looked down at her angrily. But Sandana took his hand and pulled him back onto the bench. He sat and took the sandwich she offered.

For a while they ate in silence. Then he said quietly, 'He was only a guest once. He's more of a middleman.'

Sandana placed her hand gently on his forearm. 'I'm sorry. I mean, I don't know who I'm selling tickets to either.'

'But if you did?'

Sandana pondered his question. 'I think I'd refuse.'

Maravan nodded. 'I think I would, too.'

It is possible Makeda would not have heard anything more about the Pakistan connection if Dalmann had not booked her yet again for one of his 'normal evenings at home'.

He had asked Lourdes to prepare them a cold supper for two. This usually consisted of a variety of cold meats, cold roast chicken, cooked knuckle of pork, called *gnagi*, potato salad and green salad. He would accompany this with an ice-cold table wine from the region and round it off with a few bottles of beer. Makeda stuck with champagne.

They ate in the sitting room, did not say very much, channel-hopped for a while and went to bed early.

During their TV dinner on this normal evening at home she

picked up one of the newspapers from the coffee table and leafed through it, chewing large mouthfuls of food. Without thinking, she had gone straight past the three photos. It was only a few pages later that she stopped and turned back.

She recognized two of the pictures: Carlisle and Waen. She did not recognize the third. That is to say, she had never seen the picture before, but she had seen the man. He was one of the Pakistanis from the dinner in St Moritz. Now she made out that his name was Kazi Razzaq and that he was an arms dealer.

He sold arms to the Sri Lankan army. And she had also met him at an occasion arranged by Dalmann and his strange colleague Schaeffer.

She looked at Dalmann, who was bent over on the sofa, breathing heavily as he gnawed away at his *gnagi*. 'I hope you choke on that,' she muttered.

Dalmann turned to her with a smile. 'What did you say, darling?'

'I hope you enjoy that, honey.'

Keeping to their ritual, she stood suddenly and said, 'I'll go up first.' She kissed him on the forehead, went upstairs to the bedroom and left the door slightly ajar, as if accidentally.

Dalmann followed her quietly and, through the gap in the door, watched her undress tantalizingly slowly and vanish into the bathroom, where she also left the door open. Through this he watched her shower, soap herself, rinse off, dry and moisturize herself thoroughly.

But this time she did not give him any time to scurry out of the bedroom before coming back. She suddenly stepped out of the door, dragged him by his tie to the bed, and shoved him onto the mattress. Giggling, he protested, but she did not leave him alone. 'Now you're going to get it good and proper,' she threatened, undressing him.

She gave it her best shot, and her efforts were crowned with success. But the moment Dalmann was about to penetrate her, he was let down.

She tried again: softly, roughly, intimately, affectionately and finally domineeringly and determinedly. Each time with the same result. Finally she gave up and fell into the pillows, cursing quietly. He could not understand what she had said.

Dalmann went into the bathroom, showered, and came back in pyjamas.

'These fucking pills,' he complained. 'This never used to happen to me.'

'Then just stop taking them.'

With the expert knowledge and pride of one who has survived surgery, he proceeded to tell her in detail about his stent, which enlarged the narrowed coronary vessel responsible for his heart attack, so as to prevent another blockage. And about pills and powders, which kept his blood pressure within acceptable levels, his heart beating regularly and his circulation unhindered.

Makeda listened, full of sympathy. When he had finished she said. 'Why don't we try a *Love Menu* some time?'

Why not? Dalmann thought, getting up again and fetching a goodnight beer from the fridge.

44

Maravan was sitting at his computer, trying to get through to his sister. Whenever he had to wait he would check the reports from the conflict zone. The front had declined to a tiny coastal strip on the eastern side of the island. There were around 50,000 men, women and children with the LTTE soldiers in this area. They were lacking food, water, protection from the rain, medicines and sanitary facilities. Every rocket and mortar shell was injuring and killing citizens.

Neither of the belligerents heeded the international appeals to allow safe conduct to the refugees or to limit the fighting to areas outside the densely populated refugee zone.

There were no details forthcoming about the conditions there. No journalists were allowed in the war zone.

Finally he got a connection. Maravan's sister sounded despondent and apathetic. She listed names of friends, relatives and acquaintances who were either dead or missing. The supply situation was terrible. Transports kept on being held up at checkpoints for days. Goods were being confiscated. Sea access to the peninsula was controlled by the Sri Lankan navy.

No trace of Ulagu.

She said she felt ashamed to have to ask him for money again.

He assured her that she did not need to feel ashamed. He almost added that he was ashamed enough himself.

Thevaram and Rathinam, the two LTTE men, had stopped paying unannounced visits to Maravan's flat. They could now rely on him to make donations without needing to be asked.

'You're in a difficult situation,' Thevaram had told him the last time they had met. 'You're running a catering service. For this you need a licence that you haven't got and are unlikely to get. You draw unemployment benefit, even though you earn enough, more than enough in fact. But you can't stop taking it, because you're worried the authorities would ask questions. So you're forced to take the money. Might it not unburden your conscience if you at least donated that illegally earned money to a good cause? And you'd be helping your nephew into the bargain.'

After that, whenever Maravan was paid his unemployment benefit he would deposit a sealed envelope at the Batticaloa Bazaar, addressed to Th.

Andrea knew nothing of all this. And Maravan would have continued to keep it to himself if Love Food's planning meetings had gone differently.

Yes, Andrea was now holding planning meetings. He had nothing against this; it had its advantages. It meant they did not have to discuss the calendar and bookings while preparing a dinner or in the car. But it did bother him that these meetings always took place at Andrea's flat, and that Makeda was there more often. He thought she should keep her private life and work separate, and he also found it awkward discussing financial matters in front of outsiders.

At one such meeting in the office, which was now quite homely, Andrea revealed to him that she was planning to take a fortnight's holiday with Makeda.

'Who's going to stand in for you?'

'I thought you might ask your girlfriend.'

'Sandana? Are you crazy?'

'What do you mean? She's a pretty girl and she's no fool, either.'

'She's a Tamil woman. Tamil women do not work in the sex industry.'

Up till now Makeda had been silent. But now she laughed. 'Ethiopian women don't either.'

'What about Tamil men?' Andrea asked.

'They don't either,' Maravan admitted.

'So why do you do it then?'

'Because I need the bloody money!'

Andrea got a fright; Maravan never shouted like that. 'Why don't we cancel all our bookings, then, and you take the time off too?' she suggested.

'I can't afford to,' Maravan muttered.

'But we've been earning good money. You must have put enough away for a fortnight.'

It was in response to this that Maravan disclosed his situation.

Both women listened in silence. Eventually Andrea said, 'That means you're being blackmailed.'

'Not just that. They're helping me as well.'

'How?'

Maravan told them about Ugalu. How he had signed up to be a Black Tiger and how the two men had stopped him from being accepted.

'And you believe them?' Makeda asked.

He did not reply.

'I wouldn't trust anyone who sends children to war.'

Maravan still said nothing.

'Men,' Makeda said, sticking her fingers down her throat. 'Sorry, Maravan. Men and war and money. Makes me sick.'

Andrea took her cue. 'And yet you spend all night with a man whose business contacts are flogging arms to the Liberation Tigers and the Sri Lankan army.'

Makeda stood up without saying a word and left the room. Andrea stayed seated defiantly.

'Dalmann?' Maravan asked after a while.

'Of course.'

'He's involved with the Pakistani, too?'

Andrea nodded. 'You too. You cooked for him.'

'In St Moritz.' It did not sound like a question. It was the confirmation of an unpleasant suspicion. 'But I didn't know.'

'Now you do. And so does Makeda. So what now?'

'I won't cook for him any more.'

'OK. What else?'

Makeda had come back into the room unnoticed. She was wearing her coat, scarf and gloves.

'What about you?' Andrea asked. 'What are you going to do with Dalmann now?'

'Just wait.' She kissed Andrea on the cheek, patted Maravan's head and left.

45

A cold and stormy night, rain mixed with snow. It was a five-minute walk to the tram stop. Maravan had put his hands deep into the pockets of his leather jacket, pulled his woolly hat down and hunched his shoulders.

So it was true. Dalmann was involved with people supplying arms to the army and the Liberation Tigers. Why would he have anything to do with them if he was not caught up in their deals? Sandana was right: the money he was sending his family may have been coming from the profits made by someone helping Maravan's compatriots to kill each other. And the money he sent the LTTE possibly came from the LTTE, who in turn were getting it from people like Maravan.

Everything was churning around inside his head. He had reached the tram stop, but he continued walking. The idea of sitting in a tram now, as if nothing were wrong, put him into a panic.

There was nobody on the streets. Cars drove past at long intervals. The houses were dark with closed shutters and curtains. Maravan walked quickly with long, sweeping strides. Like a criminal on the run, he thought. And he felt like one, too.

It took him almost an hour to get home, soaked through and out of breath. He lit his oil burner, put on a sarong and fresh shirt, rang the temple bell and did his *puja*.

When he had finished he knew what he had to do. The very next day he would go to Andrea and resign. It was not enough just to refuse to work for Dalmann. There were many Dalmanns in such circles. If he wanted to be sure of not getting his hands dirty he had to end it.

He would tell Thevaram and Rathinam he needed his unemployment benefit again because he was giving up his catering service with immediate effect.

It was past one o'clock in the morning, but Maravan was too unsettled to go to bed. He turned on the computer and started accessing the websites covering the civil war.

The LTTE had declared a unilateral ceasefire. The Sri Lankan defence minister called this 'a joke'. 'They should give themselves up,' he said. 'They're not fighting us, they're running away from us.'

The defence ministry website had put up a 'Final Countdown', so you could see how many square kilometres the Liberation Tigers still had to go. And the thousands of refugees packed in tightly with them. The figure was not even thirty.

One of the pro-government websites published a photo as proof that the LTTE had reneged on their promise and were still recruiting child soldiers. Two soldiers were standing in the luxuriant green of monsoon vegetation. They wore camouflage gear, had assault rifles slung over their shoulders and stared impassively at the camera. Palms and banana plants formed a dense wall in the background. A path had been cut straight through it. Tank tracks had ploughed up the soft ground.

At the soldiers' feet the bodies of four boys were leaning against an overturned tree trunk. Their heads were slumped on their shoulders as if they had nodded off. Their combat gear was of a slightly different pattern from that of the soldiers.

Maravan enlarged the picture. He let out a loud moan.

Ulagu was one of the four.

Maravan spent the rest of the night in front of his domestic shrine, praying, meditating and dozing. At half past four he sat at his monitor and dialled the number of the shop in Jaffna. It was eight o'clock there now, it would be open.

He kept on getting the message that all lines were busy and that he should try again later. After half an hour the shopkeeper answered.

Maravan asked him to send for his sister. The man would not agree until Maravan had promised him a 5,000-rupee tip when he next sent money. He should call back in two hours, he said.

They were two hours of torture. He kept on picturing Ulagu in his mind. As a frightened little boy who always needed a bit of time before he would trust somebody. As a serious young lad who never wanted to play or muck around, but just wanted to know everything about cooking. He had only ever seen Ulagu laughing when he had managed to do something difficult, while preparing food or cooking. Or when he tried something and it tasted just right.

Maravan had never met a child like Ulagu, who knew exactly what he wanted to be at such an early age – and was so convinced he would become it one day.

*

Precisely two hours later he rang again. The shopkeeper answered and put his sister on immediately.

'Ragini?'

'Yes,' she said in a muffled voice.

'Ragini,' he sobbed.

'Maravan,' she sobbed.

They wept together at a distance of 8,000 kilometres, to the static accompaniment of the World Wide Web.

46

Andrea caught up with Makeda that evening and persuaded her to come back. Maravan had already left, and they had made up. But this morning they had already started bickering again.

Andrea had made breakfast in bed and, when they had got all nice and cosy, said, 'From now on the name Dalmann is taboo, OK?'

Makeda smiled and replied, 'It's not that easy. He wants a *Love Menu*.'

Andrea looked at her, aghast.

'I hope you told him there's no way that's going to happen.'

'No, I didn't. It all goes through Kull, you know that.'

'Then *I'll* tell Kull.' Andrea had put her half-eaten croissant onto the plate and crossed her arms.

Makeda continued to eat calmly. 'He's not going to accept it just like that. Dalmann's an important client, he says. An important go-between for other clients.'

'And I'm an important service provider.'

Makeda put an arm around her. 'Come on, babe, don't be so unprofessional. He won't manage it, despite all Maravan's artistry.'

'But he'll have a go,' Andrea sulked.

'Hopefully,' Makeda said determinedly.

'What do you expect to happen?'

'That he kicks the bucket in the middle of it.'

Andrea looked at her girlfriend in horror. Makeda laughed and gave her a kiss.

At that moment the doorbell rang.

'I'm not expecting anyone.' Andrea made no move to get up.

It rang again. And again. Andrea got up in fury. She threw on her kimono and stomped to the door. 'Yes?' she barked into the intercom.

'It's me, Maravan.' He was already at the door to her flat. She opened it and let him in.

'What do you look like?'

Maravan's hair was dishevelled. He was unshaven, which, for him, meant it looked as if he had a three-day beard. Dark shadows hung below his eyes and his expression had changed. Something had been extinguished.

'What's happened?'

Instead of answering he just shook his head. 'I'm stopping,' he spluttered.

She knew exactly what he meant, but still asked, 'What do you mean, you're stopping?'

'From now on I won't be cooking for Love Food any more.'

Makeda was now standing at the bedroom door. She had wrapped a sheet around her and was smoking.

'Your nephew?' she asked.

He sunk his head.

Makeda went up to him and took him in her arms. Andrea saw his shoulders begin to twitch. The twitching spread to his back as well. Suddenly a sound burst out from his chest. A high-pitched, plaintive, drawn-out sound that seemed at odds with this tall, quiet man.

Now Makeda's expression crumpled too. Her eyes filled with tears and she buried her weeping face in his shoulder.

An hour later Maravan had calmed down enough for them to allow him to leave.

'We'll speak about stopping another time,' Andrea said at her front door.

'There's nothing more to say.'

'At least that solves the Dalmann problem,' Makeda remarked.

'What problem?'

'Dalmann wanted a *Love Menu*,' Andrea explained, 'with Makeda. At his house.'

Maravan left. But on the landing he turned round again and came back. 'After Dalmann, I'm stopping.'

47

'If someone meets an unnatural death, their restless soul has no peace and forever haunts our world as a ghost.'

'Do you believe that?' Sandana asked.

They had arrived at the highest point in the city reachable by tram and from there gone for a walk in the nearby woods. It was cold and there was snow at 800 metres. Maravan had hoped to find snow, because ever since his winter walk in the Engadin Valley he would sometimes long for that white silence. But everything was green or brown. It was only when the wind tore open the high layer of fog that he caught a glimpse of the shimmering white hills and woods.

'That's what I was taught. I never doubted our religion. I don't know anybody who does.'

'I do. If you grow up here you learn to have your doubts.'

With her quilted coat Sandana was wearing a pink woolly hat pulled down tight over her head. It made her look like a child. This impression was reinforced by the fact that, despite the seriousness of the subject they were discussing, she kept on opening her mouth wide to exhale, gazing in fascination at the cloud of steam.

Maravan thought about it. 'Must be difficult.'

'Having doubts?'

He nodded.

'Believing isn't easy either.'

An elderly couple were coming the other way. The woman had been nagging the man, but now went quiet. Maravan and Sandana interrupted their conversation as well. As they passed each other, all four of them said '*Grüezi*', according to the unwritten law of forest walkers.

They came to a fork. Without wavering Maravan plumped for the path that went upwards, towards the snow.

They continued walking at the same pace. The effort increased the gaps, first between sentences, then between individual words.

'Everyone says the war will be over soon.'

'Let's hope so,' Maravan sighed.

'Lost,' she added.

'But over at least.'

'Will you go back?'

Maravan stopped. 'In the past I was sure I would. But now, without Nangay and Ulagu . . . What about you?'

'Back? I'm from here.'

The path led to a clearing, curving slightly. When they reached the middle, they suddenly saw a deer on the path. Terrified, it turned its head towards them, then ran away. It stopped, absolutely still, at the highest point of the slope and looked down at them.

'Ulagu, maybe,' Sandana said.

He looked at her in astonishment and saw she was smiling.

He put his hands together in front of his face and bowed towards the deer. Sandana copied him.

Snow was now starting to fall from the white sky above the clearing.

April 2009

48

Some of the time-consuming things on the menu were easily prepared the day before. The erotic confectionery, for example, kept well in the fridge. Or the urad ribbons which needed time to dry and jellify. The essences from the rotary evaporator also kept well in closed, airtight jars.

Maravan was in the middle of these preparations when the doorbell rang. He opened the door. Makeda stood in the semi-darkness of the hallway, tall and smiling.

'Don't look so terrified. Nobody saw me, apart from your neighbour on the second floor.'

'That's more than enough,' he said, letting her in.

She took off her coat to reveal a traditional Ethiopian dress. 'Suits this area better, I thought.'

'What do you want?' he asked.

'I'd love some of your white tea – I don't imagine you've got any champagne in the house.'

He nodded, although this was not what he had meant, and he wondered if she had really misunderstood him. She followed him into the kitchen.

She glanced at the confectionery in various stages of completion.

'For Dalmann and me?'

Maravan nodded and filled the tea-maker with water.

'May I?' She pointed to one of the chick pea, ginger and pepper pussies yet to be glazed.

'Only one. I've made just enough.' He took two cups and saucers from a cupboard and put them on a tray.

Makeda grabbed one and bit off a piece.

The water was boiling. He poured out the tea and carried the tray into his small sitting room.

The *deepam* was burning by his domestic shrine and just for once the aroma of sandalwood was in the air. As a sacrifice to accompany his last prayer, Maravan had offered up smoke. In front of the shrine was the photo with the dead child soldiers. Makeda looked at it while Maravan set the table for the tea.

'Which one is he?'

Maravan did not look up. 'The first on the left.'

'A child.'

'He wanted to be a chef. Like me.'

'I bet he would have been a good one.'

'Definitely.' Maravan looked at the photograph. 'It's just so unfair,' he said, his voice faltering.

Makeda nodded. 'I had a cousin. She wanted to become a nurse. She was recruited when she was ten, and instead of caring for people and making them better she had to learn how to maim and kill people with a Kalashnikov. She didn't live to see her twelfth birthday.'

Now Makeda's voice was faltering too. Maravan put a hand on her shoulder.

'To a free Eritrea.' She wanted to laugh, but it sounded more like a sob.

They sat down. Both sipped carefully at the tea, which was still far too hot.

Makeda put down her cup and said. 'It's people like Dalmann who have these children on their conscience.'

Maravan shook his head slowly from side to side. 'No. It's the people who instigate these wars.'

'Those are the ideologues. They're pretty bad, too. But not as bad as the suppliers. Who make wars possible in the first place by supplying the weapons. Who make money from the war, thereby prolonging it. People like Dalmann.'

Maravan waved his hand dismissively. 'Dalmann's a small fish.'

Makeda nodded. 'Yes, but he's *our* small fish.'

Maravan said nothing.

After a long silence, Makeda said insistently, 'He stands for all the others.'

Maravan still said nothing.

'You said you wanted to stop. So why are you doing this dinner? This one in particular?'

'I don't know.'

'You're planning something, aren't you?'

'I don't know. What about you? Why are you doing it?'

'I know.'

Outside a police car siren became loud and then slowly quiet again.

'Dalmann's got a heart condition,' she said.

'Something bad I hope.'

Makeda smiled. 'He had a heart attack. They've inserted a little tube into a coronary vessel. Now he has to keep on lowering his blood pressure and thin his blood or he'll have another one.'

Maravan did not reply and blew on his tea.

'Do you know where he had it?'

Maravan shook his head.

Makeda let out her happy-go-lucky laugh, but it sounded a bit forced. 'In the Huwyler. At the busiest time.'

No reaction from Maravan.

'He needs to look after himself. Mustn't strain anything. No overdoing it.'

'I understand.'

Makeda took a gulp of her tea. 'Can you remedy erection problems too?' she asked directly.

'I think so – why?'

'Could you put something in the food to help him get an erection?'

'Not an immediate one. But in time, yes.'

'But it's got to be immediate.'

Maravan shrugged apologetically.

'There are products that work in half an hour.'

'I don't have those sorts of products.'

'I do,' Makeda said.

When she left the flat a quarter of an hour later, a foil wrap with four pills lay next to the tea service.

*

In the middle of the night Maravan awoke with a fright. He had been standing by a wall of dense, green – dark green and wet from the rain – jungle. All of a sudden tanks broke through the undergrowth, turned, cut new swathes and vanished until their diesel engines were scarcely audible. Then they came back, turned and vanished, came back, turned and vanished, until there was nothing left of the green of the jungle. In the distance he could now see the dark, calm ocean.

Maravan turned on the light. The curry plants beside his bed stood there motionless, like petrified creatures.

He looked at the clock. Three. If he did not get up now and make himself some hot milk with cardamom and turmeric, he would be unable to get to sleep again before dawn.

While he waited in the kitchen for the milk to heat up he thought about Makeda's proposition.

The milk was lukewarm by the time he had reached his decision.

49

'In the federal prosecutor's archive? Just like that? Are you taking the piss?' Already dressed for dinner, Dalmann was in his study, sitting at his desk with its brass fittings and green leather top with gold patterning. The catering team had been in the house all afternoon and he had wanted to treat himself to a small sherry before Makeda arrived. Then, all of a sudden, Schaeffer had turned up unannounced, standing there on the rug with something urgent for him.

And it really was urgent. The bunglers at the federal prosecutor's office had left lying around in some archive a whole set of copies of the so-called nuclear smuggling documents, which the Bundesrat (in a rare moment of wisdom and under pressure from the CIA) had destroyed. And instead of shredding them, as any halfway sensible person would have done, they were now shouting about them from the rooftops.

'Do we know whether they're all there? I mean, are they complete? Sod it, what I want to know is whether there's any mention of bloody Palucron.'

'Nothing that I know of. But we have to assume there is. All I know is that experts from the International Atomic Energy Agency examined the documents several days ago and they've separated the highly sensitive ones from the harmless ones.'

'I doubt Palucron will be among the highly sensitive ones.'

'For now this is what we'd like to assume.'

'So those atomic energy blokes should just take the sensitive ones and put the rest in the shredder.'

'I fear it's the sensitive ones that will be shredded.'

Dalmann took exception to his being corrected. 'So what do you suggest then, Schaeffer?' He gave his colleague a look of reproach, as if he were expecting an unforgivable mistake to be rectified immediately.

'It's still too early for any prognosis. I just wanted you to be kept informed. And I didn't want to discuss the matter over the phone, you understand.'

'You don't say! I'm already being bugged.'

'One can never be too careful where the secret services are involved.'

The doorbell rang.

'That'll be my visitor. Anything else?'

Schaeffer stood up. 'In spite of everything I hope you have a pleasant evening. Relax, I think the matter will turn out to be fairly harmless.'

'It better had,' mumbled Dalmann half-seriously. He stood up, too, and accompanied Schaeffer to the hallway, where Lourdes was helping Makeda out of her coat. Even Schaeffer seemed to notice how stunning she looked.

All afternoon Maravan had been standing in the impractical kitchen of this spacious and yet quite stuffy house. He worked with great care and concentration. He could sense clearly that

Ulagu and Nangay were in the room with him. They watched as he rattled his knife over the chopped, cored tomatoes, transformed white onions into mountains of tiny dice, removed the green shoots from garlic cloves with two cuts, worked coriander, cumin, chilli and tamarind to a fine paste. He showed them the new cooking techniques, jellification, spherification, working with foams, extracting essences. He spoke to them quietly, ignoring Andrea, who wanted to vent her bad mood on someone.

The day before, Maravan had risen early and bought some Minirin with Nangay's repeat prescription from the local chemist. The pharmacist had recognized him and asked sympathetically, 'How's your aunt? Or was it your mother?'

'Great-aunt. As well as can be expected, thank you,' Maravan had replied.

In the kitchen he had carefully studied the information leaflet, broken up one tablet and crushed it in his finest mortar. He had dabbed his moistened little finger into a few grains of the powder and tasted it. It was bitter.

He dissolved the powder in a shot glass of water. It turned milky, but soon went clear again. He sniffed it, put it back down in front of him again and started thinking.

Suddenly he stood up, went off to the grocer's in the street nearby and returned with a bottle of Campari.

He ground another pill in the mortar and dissolved it in Campari in the same shot glass. With the same result: milky at first, then clear.

Maravan filled a second glass with Campari, took a drop of each with a pipette, and tasted. Both bitter.

After that he pulverized ten times that amount and dissolved it in 150 millilitres of Campari. As soon as the liquid was clear again, he stirred in one and a half grams of alginate.

He drew up the Campari mixture into a caviar syringe and squeezed out uniform drops into a calcium chloride solution. He fished the tiny balls out of the solution, assessed, sniffed, but abstained from tasting them.

He pressed the juice of a deep-frozen orange into a fluted glass, decorated the glass with wafer-thin orange peel and let the little red balls swim in the liquid.

Maravan's Campari orange Minirin.

He took a sniff of the drink and then threw it down the sink. Again he ground tablets in the mortar. This time for the following day. Enough for three Camparis. He had heard that Dalmann was a thirsty man.

The doorbell took Maravan by surprise. If it was Makeda, she was half an hour early. But shortly afterwards Andrea came into the kitchen to give the all-clear. It was just the inevitable Schaeffer, as Andrea described him.

The doorbell rang again a good half hour later. 'There she is,' Andrea announced darkly.

Maravan prepared the aperitifs.

'Campari orange for the gentleman. And, of course, Makeda will stick to champagne.'

*

In truth, Dalmann would have preferred a normal Campari orange. Or, even better, a Campari soda. But he was not a spoilsport, never had been.

So he took the cocktail glass from the tray held by the pretty waitress and let her explain to him what the drink was. 'Campari caviar in chilled orange juice with glazed navel orange peel. Cheers.'

Dalmann waited until she had left the room, then raised his glass and toasted Makeda who, as ever, was drinking champagne. She eyed him over the rim of her glass and smiled away all his anger at the bumbling by the federal prosecutor's office.

The bedroom – or master bedroom as he called it, using the English expression – was scarcely recognizable. All the furniture had been taken out, apart from the bed and bedside table. A low, round table had been set and decorated exotically; the seating consisted of pillows and cushions.

'Oh, I see. It means you're lying down already,' he joked when they entered the room and his eyes adjusted to the candles, which provided the only lighting.

The drink tasted – funny. It was not particularly easy to drink, the swimming carpet of tiny Campari balls was slippery, either you had to slurp the things down or catch them with pursed lips. Makeda let out her infectious laugh and, to amuse her, Dalmann rather exaggerated his efforts.

Playing this game he had soon emptied his glass, and he asked, 'Do you think one might get a *supplément* of this?'

Makeda did not understand this word, and so he explained, 'Do you think I could have another one?'

She rang the temple bell.

Maravan was in the middle of preparing the *amuse-bouches*. When he opened the bottle with the curry leaf, cinnamon and coconut oil essence and drizzled a few drops onto the tiny rice-flour chapattis, the aroma of his childhood filled his nostrils once again. And Ulagu's childhood, which had ended so soon.

He did something he had never done before. He put one of the chapattis in his mouth, closed his eyes and abandoned himself to the flavour unfolding between tongue and palate.

Andrea, who was scowling by the door, waiting for the bell to ring, was watching him. 'I thought you'd made exactly the right number.'

Maravan opened his eyes, chewed, swallowed and replied, 'There'll be enough.'

The bell rang out from the first floor. Andrea grabbed the plate of chapattis and took them up the stairs.

She returned to the kitchen with a tray carrying the empty cocktail glass. 'He wants another one of those.'

Maravan mixed a second.

Dalmann enjoyed the two consistencies of urad lentil ribbons, as well as the frozen saffron and almond foam and its textures. Then Makeda came running down the stairs, ringing the temple bell loudly all the while.

'He's dying,' she said and ran back up. Maravan and Andrea followed her.

Dalmann was lying on the Indian cushions and cloths. His right hand was clutching at his chest. In the candlelight his white face had a wet sheen. His eyes were wide open in terror and he was gasping for air.

Makeda, Andrea and Maravan watched the scene from a distance. Nobody made a move to go any closer; each of them was deep in their thoughts.

Dalmann seemed to want to say something, but his struggle for air and life prevented him from doing so. At times it looked as if he was giving up; he closed his eyes and hardly breathed at all. But then he would rear up again and struggle on.

'We should call somebody,' Andrea said.

'Yes, we should,' Makeda agreed.

'144,' Maravan added.

But not one of them moved.

When the emergency services arrived, Andrea and Maravan had already gone, taking with them everything that could be linked to Love Food. Makeda had rung 144 and waited for the ambulance.

All the emergency doctor could do was confirm the patient was dead. The autopsy revealed that the stent, which had been inserted eight months previously, following his first heart attack, had become blocked, despite the fact he had been taking Aspirin Cardio and Plavix. In the doctor's opinion this unfortunate development was a result of the deceased's reckless lifestyle.

This was corroborated by the statement given by the Ethiopian-British national Makeda F., who had cooked for the deceased that evening. And also by the level of alcohol in his blood.

Hermann Schaeffer organized a suitable funeral for Eric Dalmann, which fewer mourners attended than expected. And he made sure there was a nice obituary in *Freitag*.

The other papers settled for a short announcement. Nonetheless, the name Palucron and Dalmann's connection to this firm had not yet cropped up.

On the Scilly Isles the daffodils are already in bloom in November. And now, in April, they were still in small clumps in the grass, which looked like an English lawn.

Andrea and Makeda had booked into a bed and breakfast for a fortnight. Every day they went walking on a narrow path along the coast, beside which the cliffs wallowed in the surf like sluggish, primeval creatures.

'Do you want to know why I didn't help Dalmann?' Andrea asked out of the blue. Until now they had avoided the subject.

'You wanted him to die.'

Andrea nodded. 'I was so jealous.'

Makeda put an arm around her shoulder and pulled Andrea towards her.

They continued walking for a while like this, until the path became too narrow and they had to let go of each other. Andrea went in front.

Suddenly she heard Makeda's voice behind her: 'He was supposed to have fucked himself to death.'

Andrea stopped and turned around. 'I thought he wasn't able to any more.'

'I'd planned on slipping him an erection pill.'

'How?'

'I'd asked Maravan to put it in his food.'

Andrea looked at her wide-eyed. 'So you wanted to kill him?'

Makeda nodded. 'As a representative of all those others like him.'

Andrea sat down on the soft grass beside the path. Her pale face had become even paler. 'I bet that stuff caused his heart attack.'

Makeda sat next to her and smiled. 'Definitely not. Maravan didn't mix it into the food.'

'What makes you so sure?'

'He gave me back the pills. Very discreetly that evening.'

'Thank God!'

They sat there for a while, looking out at the sea warmed by the Gulf Stream, and the clouds gathering in the west.

'Maybe there is a higher justice after all,' Andrea said thoughtfully.

'Absolutely,' Makeda replied.

50

On a platter were mango halves and pineapple boats. He had separated the mango halves very close to the core, cut diamond shapes in their dark-yellow flesh and turned them inside out. The tender flesh of the fruit now looked like a shell of sharp-edged cubes.

He had left the stiff, decorative leaves on the pineapple boats. With a sharp knife he had cut away the softest and sweetest part of the flesh from the scaly skin and sliced it straight across. This left small blocks of pineapple, which he pushed alternately to the right and left across the boat. Neither preparation was original, but they looked pretty and could be eaten by hand.

Maravan was in his own kitchen. It was early morning; it looked like rain – a cold, grey day. The dustcart had noisily emptied the bins. Once again an uncanny silence descended on the block of flats in Theodorstrasse. It had been quiet ever since the day when the Sri Lankan government had announced the defeat of the LTTE. Journalists, independent observers and aid organizations were refused entry to the war zones. There were no reliable news reports. Only rumours. Terrible rumours about 10,000 civilians killed, people starving or suffering from an epidemic, about war crimes on both sides. Those with relatives in these areas waited apprehensively for news or signs of life; those who had heard good news did not dare celebrate, out of respect for those who had heard bad. And everybody was burdened by the uncertainty of what the future had in store – for the people in Sri Lanka and those here.

Once again, however, other events ensured the drama was kept off the front pages. The top news story affected everybody. There had been an outbreak of swine flu in Mexico and the world was gripped by the fear of a pandemic like the one which had raged after the First World War, claiming millions of lives.

The evening before, Maravan had made a thick batter of rice flour, coconut milk, sugar and a little yeast, and allowed it to ferment overnight. Half an hour ago he had added some salt and baking powder. Now it was time to coat the small, hot, semi-circular iron pan with a little coconut oil.

He put it back on the heat, dropped in two dessertspoons of batter, took the pan by its handle from the cooker and let its contents run to form a layer at either side. He cracked open an egg and poured it into the middle of the batter. Then he returned the pan to a low flame and covered it. Three minutes later the edges of the hopper were brown and the egg was cooked through. He kept the egg hopper warm in the oven and started making the next one.

When he brought the tray with the aromatic hoppers, coconut chutney, tea and fruit into the bedroom it was still dark.

But Sandana's voice sounded clear and awake when she said, 'So, when are you going to cook *me* a love menu?'

'Never.'

Maravan's Recipes

Maravan's recipes are partly inspired by Heiko Antoniewicz's wonderful cookbook *Verwegen kochen: Molekulare Techniken und Texturen* (Matthaes Verlag). In the following collection of recipes, Antoniewicz has simplified the preparation and, where we thought necessary, allowed the dishes to be made with less elaborate kitchen equipment. The amounts specified for the *Love Menu* recipes are for a ten-course meal for two people. Those for the *Promotional Menu* are for four people.

The Love Menu

Mini chapattis with essence of curry leaf, cardamom and coconut oil
Urad lentil ribbons in two consistencies
Ladies' fingers curry on sali rice with garlic foam
Poussin curry on sashtika rice with coriander foam
Churaa varai on nivara rice with mint foam
Frozen saffron and almond foam with saffron textures
Sweet and spicy spheres of cardamom, cinnamon and ghee
Glazed chickpea, ginger and pepper vulvas
Jellied asparagus and ghee phalluses
Liquorice, honey and ghee ice lollies

*

Mini chapattis with essence of curry leaf, cardamom and coconut oil

Mini chapattis
65g wheat flour
40ml lukewarm water
1 tsp ghee

Work the flour and water by hand into a very smooth dough, kneading for about 8 minutes. Cover the dough with a muslin cloth and leave to rest for 1 hour. With floured hands make marble-sized balls of dough. Sprinkle a work surface with a little flour, flatten the dough balls and roll them into thin rounds. Just before serving, dry fry them on both sides in a hot cast-iron pan until brown.

Essence of curry leaf, cardamom and coconut oil

100g coconut oil
9 fresh curry leaves
1 cinnamon stick, coarsely ground

Put all the ingredients for about 1 hour in a rotary evaporator at 55°C. For the essence you can use either the distillate from the upper flask or the concentrate from the lower one. Maravan mixes the two. Drip the essence onto the chapattis using a pipette.

Urad lentil ribbons in two consistencies

200g dal lentils
150ml milk
50g yoghurt
70g rock sugar
2g agar agar

Leave the lentils to soak in the sugared milk for at least 6 hours. Blend to a fine paste. Spread half of this onto a baking sheet, cut lengthways into strips, and dry in the oven at 50°C. Remove from baking sheet while still warm and twist into the desired shape.

Mix the other half of the paste with agar agar and heat to 90°C. Stir in the yoghurt, then also spread thinly onto a baking sheet. Leave to cool and cut into strips of the same width as the others. Intertwine with the dried spirals before serving.

Ladies' fingers curry on sali rice with garlic foam

Ladies' fingers curry
10 tender okra pods (ladies' fingers)
2 green chillies, finely chopped
1 medium onion, finely chopped
¼ tsp fenugreek seeds
½ tsp chilli powder
½ tsp salt
5–8 fresh curry leaves
50ml water
50ml thick coconut milk

Wash the okra and leave to dry or pat with kitchen paper. Cut into 3cm pieces. In a saucepan mix the okra, chilli, onion and all the spices thoroughly. Add the water and cook until almost all the liquid has evaporated. Stir and add the coconut milk. Cook for a further 3 minutes. Reduce the liquid on a low heat.

Sali rice

1 cup sali rice
2 cups water
salt

Briefly pan fry the rice and add the water. Cover and leave to cook for about 20 minutes in the oven at 160°C. Remove from oven and immediately break up the rice with a wooden spatula so that it doesn't stick. Put into a form and keep warm. When needed, remove from the form and place the curry on top.

Garlic foam

200ml chicken stock, all fat removed
1 clove garlic
1 dash lemon juice
2g soya lecithin

Blend the stock finely with the other ingredients and pass through a sieve. Combine with the soya lecithin, season and whisk. Cover a large bowl with some clingfilm to prevent splashing, and under this whisk up the foam, working in plenty of air. Leave to settle for a while. Using a slotted spoon remove the foam and arrange as desired.

Poussin curry on sashtika rice with coriander foam

Poussin curry
200g poussin, cut into bite-size pieces
3½ tsp coriander seeds
½ tsp cumin seeds
½ tsp black pepper
1 dried red chilli
1 large onion, chopped
¼ tsp fenugreek seeds
1 pinch turmeric powder
6 cloves garlic
salt according to taste
400ml water

½ tsp tamarind paste
6–8 fresh curry leaves
1 dessertspoon thick coconut milk

Finely grind the coriander and cumin seeds, pepper and chillies. Simmer the poussin, onion, fenugreek seeds, turmeric, garlic and salt in 300ml water, covered. Dissolve the ground spice mixture and tamarind in 100ml water and add, together with the curry leaves and coconut milk. Bring to the boil, simmer for 2 minutes and remove from the heat.

Sashtika rice

1 cup sashtika rice
3 cups water
Salt

Prepare as for sali rice above.

Coriander foam

200ml chicken stock, all fat removed
20 coriander seeds
1 bunch coriander leaves
2g soya lecithin

Prepare as for garlic foam above.

Churaa varai on nivara rice with mint foam

Churaa varai
250g shark steak
200g shredded coconut
¼ tsp turmeric powder
½ tsp ground pepper
1 tsp ground cumin
1 tsp salt
¼ tsp chilli powder (or according to taste)
1½ dessertspoons coconut oil
1 large onion, chopped
4 dried red chillies
½ tsp mustard seeds
9–11 fresh curry leaves

Steam the shark steak and leave to cool. Flake and mix thoroughly with the coconut, turmeric, pepper, cumin, salt and (according to taste) chilli powder. Sweat the onion in a pan with coconut oil until translucent. Add the dried chillies, mustard seeds and curry leaves, and fry until the mustard seeds start to jump. Add the shark mixture and stir everything together thoroughly on a low heat.

Nivara rice

1 cup nivara rice
3 cups water
salt

Prepare as for sali rice above.

Mint foam

200ml chicken stock, fat removed
1 bunch mint, leaves picked from stems
A little low-fat milk
2g soya lecithin

Prepare as for garlic foam above.

Frozen saffron and almond foam with saffron textures

Saffron textures
200ml mineral water
80g rock sugar, powdered
2g saffron powder
2g saffron threads
2g agar agar
1 leaf gelatine, soaked and squeezed out
40g ghee

Heat the water with the rock sugar. Dissolve the saffron powder in the water and stir in the agar agar. Bring to the boil and add the gelatine. Pour onto warmed plastic trays and leave to cool. Cut into 2cm wide strips. Brush with a thin covering of ghee and arrange the saffron threads on top. Roll up and arrange the cylinders on the plate so that they flank the foam.

Frozen saffron and almond foam

300ml cream
3g saffron powder
140g grated almonds
2 egg whites
1 dessertspoon rock sugar, powdered
2g salt

Heat the cream to 60°C and thoroughly blend all the ingredients except the egg whites. Add the egg whites, put everything into a 0.5l siphon, spray using a nitrogen cartridge, and chill for 3 hours. If required put nitrogen into a Dewar flask and chill a metal spoon. Spray a walnut-sized ball of foam onto the spoon and turn for 20 seconds in the nitrogen bath. Arrange between the saffron textures and serve immediately.

Sweet and spicy spheres of cardamom, cinnamon and ghee

Spice paste
200ml coconut water
40g ghee
2 spikes long pepper
1 cardamom pod
1 pinch cinnamon powder
40g palm sugar
0.5g xanthan gum
2g calcium lactate

In a mortar pound the ghee and spices to a fine paste. Warm the paste, pass through a sieve and mix with the texturizers in the coconut water. Leave to rest until the air bubbles have disappeared. Gently heat before using.

Brine

500ml mineral water
2.5g alginate

Mix the two ingredients and leave to stand.

Using a round spoon make balls from the spice paste in the brine. Draw some warmed ghee into a disposable syringe and affix a needle. Inject the spheres in the brine with ghee, retract the needle, then turn the spheres immediately so that the pricks close up. Leave for 3 to 5 minutes in the brine. Rinse with water and keep warm at 60°C under clingfilm.

Glazed chickpea, ginger and pepper vulvas

50g sali rice
300ml milk
2 dessertspoons chickpea flour
1 dessertspoon ghee
2 dessertspoons palm sugar
1 dessertspoon chopped almonds
1 dessertspoon raisins
3 dates
½ teaspoon powdered ginger
½ teaspoon milled black pepper

Steep the rice in milk and blend, adding milk all the while, until you have a fine, moist paste. Add a further 150ml milk and stir well. Pass everything through a fine muslin and squeeze out well. Add another 50ml of milk to the extract. Fry the chickpea flour in ghee, boil it up in the liquid together with the sugar and stir continuously on a low heat, working it to a viscous mixture. Add the remaining ingredients and keep stirring for another 2–3 minutes on a low heat. Spread the paste onto a baking sheet and leave to cool. Cut up into equal portions, form the desired shape and glaze. Dry in the oven at 60ºC.

Glaze

100g icing sugar
1 dessertspoon pomegranate syrup

Mix the ingredients and glaze the biscuits. Allow to dry to a matt sheen.

Jellied asparagus and ghee phalluses

(This recipe uses fresh asparagus. Maravan uses dried asparagus, reducing the liquid in the rotary evaporator.)

200g white asparagus
1 dessertspoon sugar
A little salt
4g agar agar
1 leaf gelatine, soaked and squeezed out
1g chlorophyll
4 cardamom pods, finely ground
100g ghee

Put the asparagus in a saucepan with cold water, cover and bring to the boil. Add cardamom and cook until the asparagus is tender. Purée the asparagus and pass through a sieve. Put 4 dessertspoons of the mixture to one side and mix with the chlorophyll. Mix 3g of the agar agar with the rest of the purée, bring to the boil and add the gelatine. Pour into a flat form and chill until the mass is workable. Cut into strips, roll these in baking paper and chill. When these have set, roll into sausages and cut into 10-cm long pieces. Boil up the rest of the asparagus with 1g agar agar. Dip one end of each jellied asparagus into the pan to a depth of 2cm several times until a green bulge is formed. Chill. Cut the green heads with small scissors so that they look like asparagus tips. Serve with a small bowl of warm cardamom, chilli and ghee dip.

Liquorice, honey and ghee ice lollies

100ml water
20g liquorice paste
30g honey
30g ghee
0.5g xanthan gum
40g pistachios, cut into thin slices

Heat the water. Stir in the honey and liquorice paste. Mix in the *xanthan* and stir the ghee into the warm mixture. Pour circles of the mixture onto a sheet lined with baking paper, and give each one a wooden stick. Sprinkle with the pistachios and freeze. Take from freezer and serve when required.

The Promotional Menu

Cinnamon curry caviar chapattis

Baby snapper marinated in turmeric with molee curry sabayon

Frozen mango curry foam

Milk-fed lamb cutlets in jardaloo essence with dried apricot purée

Beech-smoked tandoori poussin on tomato, butter and pepper jelly

Kulfi with mango air

*

Cinnamon curry caviar chapattis

(Made without using rotary evaporator)
40ml mineral water
4 fresh curry leaves
1 cinnamon stick
1 pinch sugar
1 pinch salt
120ml coconut water
1g alginate
2g calcium chloride
500ml water
10g coconut oil

Briefly heat the water. Add the spices and leave to infuse for 1 hour. Add salt and sugar. Strain through a fine muslin, squeezing well. The liquid should give 20ml of essence. Mix with the coconut water and season to taste. Blend the alginate with a wand mixer. Leave until all air bubbles have disappeared. Mix the chloride with the water and put to one side. Put the curry mixture into a large syringe and squirt drops into the brine. Leave for a maximum of 1 minute and rinse in water. Drain well and serve quickly so that the balls do not set in the centre. Arrange on the warm chapattis and grate a little coconut oil on top.

Baby snapper marinated in turmeric with molee curry sabayon

Baby snapper marinated in turmeric

4 boneless baby snapper fillets
1 pinch turmeric
salt
60ml liquid coconut milk
juice and zest of 1 lime

Make a few cuts in the fillets and arrange in a form. Blend the other ingredients with a wand mixer and put on top of the fish. Marinate for at least 6 hours in the refrigerator. Take out and pat dry. Starting with the head end, roll up the fillets and fix them with wooden skewers. Bake for 12–15 minutes on a lightly oiled sheet in a fan-assisted oven at 60°C, so that the fillets are still slightly translucent.

Molee curry sabayon

1 small onion, finely diced
1 small chilli, deseeded and very finely chopped
1 clove garlic, finely chopped
10g diced ginger
20g coconut oil
1 fully ripe tomato
5 crushed peppercorns
2 crushed cloves
1 cardamom pod
4 curry leaves

Baby snapper marinade

300ml fish stock
50ml coconut oil
1g xanthan gum
1g guar gum

Sweat the onion with the other spices in the coconut oil until translucent. Quarter the tomatoes and add to the pan. Fry until the spices have fully opened up their aroma. Pour on the marinade, bring to the boil and reduce slightly. Add the fish stock and reduce again in a water bath to 300ml. Strain through a fine sieve and mix with the coconut oil. Blend the *xanthan* gum and guar gum with a wand mixer. Put into a 0.5l siphon, spray using a nitrogen cartridge and keep warm at 60°C in a water bath. Put the fillets on the plates and arrange with the sabayon from the siphon.

Frozen mango curry foam

200g mango purée
150g cream
20g chickpea flour
10ml ginger juice
1 pinch chilli powder
1 pinch cumin powder
1 pinch Kashmir curry powder

(Maravan fries the spices individually and then grinds them to make his own curry powder.)

Briefly blend all the ingredients, pass through a fine sieve and place into a 0.5l siphon spray using a nitrogen cartridge and chill. If desired, the foam can also be sprayed onto a metal spoon cooled in nitrogen and turned in nitrogen for a maximum of 20 seconds. Serve immediately.

Milk-fed lamb cutlets in jardaloo essence with dried apricot purée

Milk-fed lamb cutlets in jardaloo essence
2 lamb cutlets with bones
200ml lamb stock
2 onions, finely diced
20g ginger, finely diced
2 cloves garlic, finely grated
2 cinnamon sticks
1 small chilli, mashed
A little cumin
1 dessert spoon ghee

Sweat the onions in the ghee and add the spices. Fry gently until the oils are released and give off their aroma. Add the lamb stock and reduce everything by half in a water bath. Finely strain the stock and put with the lamb cutlets in a vacuum pack. Cook in a water bath at 65°C for 15 minutes, remove the cutlets, pat dry and fry briefly.

Dried apricot purée

100g stoned unsulphured dried apricots
50ml orange juice
1 dessertspoon white wine vinegar
100g softened onions

Soak the apricots in the orange juice and wine vinegar. Heat up with the onions and work to a fine purée. Put the purée on the plates and arrange the sliced lamb cutlets. Add the potatoes and pour around some of the cooking liquid.

Beech-smoked tandoori poussin on tomato, butter and pepper jelly

Beech-smoked tandoori poussin
2 boned poussins
1 clove garlic, grated
10g ginger, finely chopped
1 chilli, finely chopped
8 ground coriander seeds
1 pinch garam masala
salt
Juice and zest of 1 lemon
30g yoghurt

Place the poussins in a vacuum bag. Make a fine paste out of the other ingredients and add to the poussins. Close the bag and poach for 20 minutes in a water bath at 65°C. Remove the poussins and fry briefly.

Tomato, butter and pepper jelly

100ml tomato juice
100ml red pepper juice
20g ghee
2g agar agar
1 tsp beechwood smoking sawdust

Blend the juices with the ghee and the agar agar. Bring to the boil and pour into a rectangular form. Chill for two hours and cut into pieces of the desired size. Warm in the oven at 90°C.

Put the poussins in petri dishes and arrange the jelly. Add some of the poaching liquid. Burn the smoking sawdust in an electric pipe and pass the smoke under the petri dishes. Serve immediately, smoking for a maximum of 1 minute.

Kulfi with mango air

Kulfi

100ml milk
100ml cream
40g sugar
A little lime juice
1 pinch cardamom
1g saffron

Heat the milk to 60°C and dissolve the sugar in it. Stir in the lime juice, cardamom and saffron. Mix with the cream and season to taste. Using a whisk, beat the mixture with nitrogen in a coated vessel to a creamy ice and immediately form into balls.

Mango air

200ml mango juice
a little lime juice
2g soya lecithin
4 leaves of silver leaf

Mix all the ingredients together and whisk in air with a wand mixer. Wait until the foam has stabilized and then remove. Serve with the ice cream with the silver leaf.

Bibliography

Heiko Antoniewicz, *Fingerfood: Die Krönung der kulinarischen Kunst* (Stuttgart: Matthaes, 2006)

Heiko Antoniewicz and Klaus Dahlbeck, *Molekulare Basics: Grundlagen und Rezepte* (Stuttgart: Matthaes, 2008)

'Chronik einer beispiellosen Krise', DRS24 News (http://www.drs4news.ch)

Chandra Dissanayake, *Ceylon Cookery* (Colombo: Felix Printers, 1968)

Nesa Eliezer, *Recipes of the Jaffna Tamils* (Hyderabad: Orient Longham Private Ltd, 2003)

Vera Markus, *In der Heimat ihrer Kinder* (Zürich: Offizin, 2005)

Camellia Panjabi, *Currys – Das Herz der indischen Küche* (Munich: Christian Verlag, 1996)

Vinod Verma, *Ayurveda for Life: Nutrition, Sexual Energy and Healing* (York Beach, ME: Weiser Books, 1997)

Thomas Vilgis, *Die Molekularküche* (Wiesbaden: Tre Torri, 2007)

Acknowledgements

I should like to thank Heiko Antoniewicz for his advice and experience, for having read through and made corrections to the text, and for having produced recipes for these dishes. Thanks to Lathan Suntharalingam for his advice on all matters relating to the Tamil situation and Tamil culture. Thanks to my friend Prof. Dr Hans Landolt from Aarau Canton Hospital for the gruesome medical advice. Thanks to Frau Irene Tschopp and Herr Can Akrikan from the Office for Business and Employment at the Economic Directorate of Zürich Canton, Frau Bettina Dangel from the Migration Office of Zürich Canton, Herr Beat Rinz from Zürich Unemployment Office, the Commissariat for Police Authorizations at Zürich City Police, and the Zürich Food Safety Authority for their friendly and unbureaucratic answers to my questions. Thanks are due to Herr Simon Plüss, departmental head of export controls and munitions of the State Secretariat for Economic Affairs (SECO), for the detailed and thorough information he provided. Many thanks to Frau Vera Markus for her help and her book *In der Heimat ihrer Kinder*, and to Frau Paula Lanfranconi and Frau Damaris Lüthi for their expert contributions to this work. Thanks also to Herr Andreas Weibel from the Group for a Switzerland without an Army (GSoA) for the insightful information on the situation relating to weapons exports from Switzerland.

I should like to thank my friend and reader Ursula Baumhauer for her assistance, which, as ever, was professional, purposeful and enjoyable. Thanks to my children Ana and Antonio for their small interruptions during my work on this book. Thanks to my wife Margrith Nay Suter for her unerring, precise and creative criticism. Thanks, finally, to Diogenes Verlag for their support at a difficult time.

Note on the Author

Martin Suter was born in Zurich in 1948. His novels have enjoyed huge international success and have been published in twenty-nine languages. He is married and, with his family, he spends his time between Spain and Guatemala.